THE LOVE OF ANNIE

GLADYS ZELLGERT

WINEPRESS WP PUBLISHING

© 1999 by Gladys Zellgert. All rights reserved

Printed in the United States of America

Packaged by WinePress Publishing, PO Box 428, Enumclaw, WA 98022. The views expressed or implied in this work do not necessarily reflect those of WinePress Publishing. Ultimate design, content, and editorial accuracy of this work are the responsibilities of the author.

No part of this publication may be reproduced, stored in a retrieval system, or transmitted in any way by any means—electronic, mechanical, photocopy, recording, or otherwise—without the prior permission of the copyright holder, except as provided by USA copyright law.

Unless otherwise noted all verses marked KJV are taken from the King James Version of the Bible.

ISBN 1-57921-225-5
Library of Congress Catalog Card Number: 99-63386

I dedicate this book
in loving memory
of my mother,
Annie DeVault.

Acknowledgments

I wish to thank first of all, my husband, Victor Zellgert, who without his patience and support, I could not have written this book.

I also wish to thank my children: Victor Zellgert Jr., and his wife Judi; and my daughter Kathleen, and her husband Dennis Neuberger, for their encouragement and help along the way and for always being there for me when I needed support.

A big thank you to my sisters Ruth Jones, Elsie Smith, and Ethel Smallwood, who helped me to compile the needed information. Their help with the research into the life of Annie is truly appreciated.

A special thank you to my great-grandchild James, who at only five years of age, helped to get me through a hurdle on my computer, as I was just a beginner in the computer world.

This book is based on a true story.
Some of the names have been changed
to protect the persons involved.

Chapter 1

"Annie," she said, "I heard you crying last night. Did Bronson hurt you?"

Not wanting to cause any trouble, Annie denied it, ate her breakfast, then started her chores. She was so frightened; she knew she would cry if she talked about it. She feared that if Bronson found out she had told his mother how he treated her, he would abuse her even more. She decided not to say anything at all and to pretend everything was going along fine.

Annie knew that marrying Bronson was what her mother wanted her to do. So did Bronson! With so much pressure, it was easier for her to do what Bronson and her mother wanted, rather than to continue to resist, even though she was barely fifteen years old.

When her mother brought up the subject of marriage again and again, Annie told her, "I am frightened and skeptical of what my future would be with him."

"Nonsense, Annie. He is a fine gentleman. Well bred and comes from a good family, so quit fretting about him."

"Mama, Bronson gets upset when other boys even speak to me. He demands that I stay by him constantly and doesn't want me to talk to them, especially Howard, a boy who comes to the parties while visiting his relatives. He treats everyone nice, and Bronson doesn't like him."

"Perhaps he is displaying a little jealousy," was her mother's reply.

Annie was young and innocent. The thought of the new boy being anything more than a nice man never entered her mind. She was a beautiful brown-eyed girl, very kind and gentle. She had a lovely disposition. Everyone liked her. When people met her the first time, they seemed in awe of her beauty and her happy personality. Young men found her both witty and beautiful. This combination, along with her kind, thoughtful ways, tended to turn young men's heads. They immediately took a liking to her and would sit for hours listening to her talk about the Shenandoah Valley in Virginia where she was raised.

Her grandparents had slaves, and it bothered her to think that slaves were taken from their homes. Even as a small child she had a hard time accepting the fate of these people. She would talk to strangers or anyone who would listen to her about the treatment of them. Her friendly ways worried her mother.

Annie's mother realized when Annie was a young child this certain quality she had. Each year her inner beauty grew, along with her physical beauty. Her mother constantly worried that something would happen to Annie, since everywhere she went, she drew attention. She stood out amongst people more than her sisters did. This is perhaps why her mother wanted Annie to settle down early in her young life.

Annie began to think her mother didn't care about her feelings or her life at all. Of course, this is what Bronson wanted. He would tell Annie that he cared for her more then her mother cared. Annie knew her mother favored her sisters much more than her. Thinking she couldn't please her mother, she believed Bronson and agreed to marry him.

Of course, Bronson insisted they marry as soon as possible. He wanted to be sure Annie would not have time to change her mind. So they went across the state line to be married.

For a young innocent girl like Annie, the marriage seemed exciting. They lived with Bronson's parents, and everything seemed good. Annie thought she must have made the right decision. She felt more relaxed, since the pressure was no longer on her as before.

Not long after getting settled, Annie noticed Bronson seemed to be getting more self-centered and demanding. He found fault with her every move. He wanted her to be there every minute, although she had work to do. Annie felt she should be of some help to Bronson's mother, since they were living with her. But he wanted her for himself and always demanded she quit whatever she was doing to be with him and do as he commanded. The love he had shown her before their marriage suddenly changed. His lovemaking was for his own satisfaction. It did not matter how Annie felt. He did not care. He began to show sadistic traits. Under the pretense of love, he pinched and bit her. Annie, not having anyone she could talk to, tried to hide her fears, but each night his biting and pinching seemed to get worse.

Finally, it became so bad, Annie dreaded to see the darkness of night close in around her, and she would have to be alone with him. In the daytime, Bronson seemed kind and gentle. His mother didn't know the torture and pain her son inflicted upon Annie in the quiet of their bedroom. Living with Bronson's mother made Annie feel even worse. She was very fond of her and did not want to cause her any grief, so she tried to keep this problem to herself.

Before Bronson and Annie were married, they had attended church regularly, but now that came to a sudden stop. Bronson only did what he wanted to do and expected Annie to do the same. He would no longer go to church at all. To keep peace between them, she, too, stayed away from going, with the hope that he would know she was trying to please him and that he would be gentler with her.

One night, when the biting was so painful, Annie began to cry. This angered Bronson to the point he really abused her. "Shut up! I am not hurting you! If you want attention, I'll give you some. Now don't be bawling anymore."

"Bronson, oh, Bronson, why are you being so rude? You were always so kind and such a gentleman when we were just seeing each other. Now, . . . now you hurt me, and you won't stop! Why Bronson? Why have you changed? I thought you really cared for me."

"I do care for you, but now you belong to me, and you will do as I say."

Annie could not stop crying. When she cried aloud, it woke Bronson's mother. His mother tiptoed up the stairs and stood outside their door. She could hear Annie sobbing. She also heard Bronson's threats to bite her some more if she did not quiet herself. His mother remained very quiet, not knowing just how to handle this awful treatment that her son was inflicting upon Annie. As if in a trance, she thought to herself, *This can not go on any longer. I must find a way to help her.* As Bronson's mother waited outside the door she heard a noise. She knew it was Annie. She stood very quietly, deciding if she should go inside and put a stop to this nonsense or wait a little longer to be sure this was the right thing for her to do.

Annie muffled her cry, and after what seemed forever, Bronson fell asleep.

When it got quiet, Bronson's mother tiptoed down the stairs. It disturbed her to think that her only son could be this mean and treat Annie so badly.

Annie lay quietly, trying to think of a way to get away from Bronson and go back to the valley where she had lived before marrying him. The bleak feeling of being trapped, with no one to help her, was all she could think of. Not wanting Bronson to wake up, she lay ever so still, in fear that if he awakened, she would have to endure more pain.

Each night became a nightmare with the pain, the torture, and his mocking when she cried. Annie began staying up later and later before going to bed, pretending she had things to do. She worked hard to prolong the time before she had to go to her room and be with him. Yet the fear of him getting angrier because she had lingered too long in the kitchen, was almost as bad.

As Annie was trying to find things to do to keep from being with Bronson, she often thought back to how different it was when she was dating him. How gentle he had been and how much he had loved her. She also thought of her mother. She knew her mother thought Bronson was a gentleman, and she would never conceive of him doing such a thing as this to her.

The Love of Annie

Annie would also think of her father, how years ago he had listened to stories over and over again about the Ohio Valley. Many times he thought he'd like to settle down there. She remembered how her father's face lit up when talking of the beautiful Ohio Valley.

Annie's thoughts went back to the time she wandered off into the valley to watch the water rushing through the rocks and disappearing into the woods. She was late getting home, and her mother was so frightened something had happened to her, she became very upset.

Her mother got herself under control again. Thinking she was calm, she decided to give Annie a haircut. Not realizing she was still so emotional, she did a poor job in cutting Annie's hair. She had to shave her little head bald so the hair would grow out more evenly. Annie remembered how sad she felt when she looked in the mirror and saw her hair had been cut off, and how angry and ashamed it made her feel knowing she had to face her friends at school. Her aunt felt sorry for Annie, so she made her two little bonnets to wear to school, with the hope that the children wouldn't tease her. This thought brought a tiny smile to her lips. She had cried so much, her mother sent her to her room without supper.

Annie's brother Guy loved her, and it bothered him to see her go to bed without eating. Annie smiled a little again when she thought of her brother Guy. They were very close to each other.

These thoughts of days gone by were happy thoughts. Thinking of school days with her friends always made Annie happy. She loved going to school and remembered all too clearly how she wished she could go on to further her education, but the sixth grade was all that was available to her.

All too soon, Annie realized she had stayed up much too long, and she hurriedly went up the stairs to her bedroom, dreading the thought of facing Bronson again.

After Bronson left bruises all over her face and body one night, Annie came down for breakfast. Just one quick look at her told Bronson's mother that she had to do something to get her away from him. There was no mistaking the cruelty he inflicted upon her.

She took Annie's hand gently, drew her aside, and whispered, "Annie, I heard you crying and sobbing again last night. This just absolutely can not go on. Oh my, what is wrong with that boy? You can't live like this. You are much too nice to have to put up with this type of cruelty. I will help you to get away from him." Bronson's mother told her, "I love you so much, honey, but you must get away from him, and fast, before he hurts you even more. I will help you. I know Bronson has to go to town for supplies tomorrow morning. You go now and pack your belongings. Bring them to my room so that he won't notice your baggage or get suspicious that you are leaving him. Now go, child, and hurry before he comes in. You must get away from him!"

Annie hurriedly gathered up her things and took them to hide in his mother's room, fearing every moment that Bronson would come in before she had her clothes packed and hidden where he would not see them. Annie, knowing they would leave early in the morning after Bronson had left to get his supplies, felt a surge of relief. The happy thought of not hurting anymore, of only one more night to endure his attacks (not a happy thought) made her heart pound hard and fast. She was excited that she would get away and go back to her home in the valley.

The Love of Annie

Annie dressed for bed that night in the prettiest nightgown she had, hoping he would think she dressed to please him and perhaps be gentler with her. The sight of her in the low cut neckline, however, seemed to make his attacks all the worse. He kept taunting her, "You belong to me! You are not crying. You can quit your pretending. I know you enjoy being with me. You have to realize I am the best of all the others who asked you to go out. By the way, Annie, just why didn't you ever date other men? Oh well, that's not important, let's get back to what is important. Now where were we? Annie, I told you to quit that pretending, for heaven's sake. You are not crying; you are beginning to like it."

Over and over again Annie begged Bronson to be a little more gentle, but her begging was all in vain. His selfishness was uncontrollable. Oh, how she wanted to cry, even more so than before, since the pain was near the point of being unbearable. All the more, she fought to hold back the tears, anything, so that he would not suspect that she was leaving him in the morning.

Finally, . . . finally . . . it's all over, she thought as she lay on her pillow, waiting for him to go to sleep, which he did, and not any too soon. How she wished the hours would pass much more quickly. To her, the time passed by so slowly; it seemed to be standing still.

Knowing that this was her last frightful night there, she could not relax. She looked at Bronson again to be sure he was asleep. She feared he was just pretending, and she had to be sure before she could calm down enough to get some rest.

The thought of being free from him excited her. The very thought of morning coming, and she being safe again, sent a happy sensation through her tiny body. The fear that something might go awry, and that Bronson might find out she was leaving him and not let her go, was so frightening, she shuddered at the very thought of it. She tried ever so hard to dispel that thought. The mere thought of that happening made her tremble. Closing her eyes, she asked God to calm her, so she would not wake Bronson.

 Morning came all too slowly. At last Bronson hitched up the horses and was off on his journey to buy supplies. A powerful relief came over Annie as he drove out of the barnyard and out of her life.

Chapter 2

With breakfast over, and Bronson gone, his mother and Annie hurried to put Annie's baggage into the buggy. Bronson's mother wanted to get started on their way, so they would be sure to be gone if, by chance, Bronson came back sooner than expected. He would most certainly be even angrier if he knew that his own mother helped Annie to get away from him.

They arrived at Annie's home a few hours later. Annie's mother was ashamed and very sad to have made such a mistake that caused so much trouble. "Annie, I am truly sorry. I honestly thought Bronson was a true gentleman. I feel bad that I was so set in my own way that you should marry him. Now look at the heartbreak I have caused you."

"Mama, don't feel so bad. I am so happy to be here. Being home again is what is important. I am home now, and that is all that matters."

"I am also sorry to have put you through so much trouble," Annie's mother said, apologizing to Bronson's mother. "I felt so strongly they would be happy together."

"It was no trouble. I am happy that I realized the dilemma Annie was in and I could help her to get away. I love Annie so much. I am going to miss her. I could not let that kind of abuse go on any longer."

Bronson's mother held Annie very gently and said, "I will always love you, Annie, but I could not stand to see you being hurt over and over again. Someday you will find someone who won't hurt you. Someone who will love you and be good to you, and some day maybe . . . just maybe," she said with a wistful look in her eyes, "we will see you again."

She kissed Annie on her forehead and held her close for a long time. With tears in her eyes, she turned and walked away, turning slightly to say, "I love you, Annie. I will always love you." Then hurriedly, she climbed into the buggy.

Annie was happy that she was free, and, yet, a little sad at the thought she may never see Bronson's mother again. She ran to the buggy. "Thank you, oh, thank you, for bringing me home. I am so grateful to you. Goodbye," she whispered. "I love you for being so kind. Please get back safely," Annie said, sadly.

Bronson's mother said a faint goodbye as she turned the corner and rode out of sight. Out of Annie's life, into the shadows of the night.

As Annie walked back her mother noticed the bruises on her face. "What happened, Annie? Did Bronson do this to you?" she gasped. "I never thought he could be so cruel. I'm sorry. I am so sorry. He always seemed so nice. I'm glad you are back home again."

"I'm all right, Mama. It's all over, and I'm so glad to be home," Annie replied. She ran into her mother's arms. After a long embrace, tears ran down Annie's face, but this time they were tears of happiness.

Oh what a glorious feeling it gave Annie to be back with Guy and her sisters, back to the safety of her home once more.

There was so much for them to talk about; midnight came all too soon. As Annie climbed the steps to her room and then nestled under the covers, the warmth and peaceful feeling of not being afraid brought her such ecstasy. After such a nightmare she had been put through, this tremendous, joyous feeling was almost more than she could have hoped for. Knowing and feeling the safety of her own bed again gave her such a warm, happy, and peaceful feeling. For a few minutes she lay there wondering how she could possibly have made such a mistake to have married a man who was so nice when she was going with him, then so cruel after being married such a short time. She lay only a few minutes, knowing her fears were behind her, and then fell asleep from sheer exhaustion.

When Annie awoke the next morning, her whole world seemed much brighter. The grass looked greener, and the sun seemed to smile down upon her. "Home," she said to herself, "I can't believe I am home and safe from Bronson's attacks and the cruel treatment he inflicted upon me. In only such a short period of time, it does not seem possible that any one could be so nice, then change to that degree so quickly."

She could hardly wait to go down for breakfast. Being back in her old routine again, seemed almost too good to be true. *Those couple of months of being married to Bronson seemed like a lifetime, or more like a bad nightmare,* she thought as she dressed for breakfast, trembling and shaking so badly, she could barely get herself dressed. *I must get hold of myself. It is all over, so calm down,"* she said to herself. "I must forget all that I have been through. The very thought of him sent chills through her tiny body.

Putting the thought out of her mind, she pulled herself together. She had her future to think about now. She was very determined to start her life all over again and to prove she would not let Bronson ruin the rest of her young life. *This won't be easy for me to do,* she thought, *knowing how little it takes for me to shake at the mere thought of Bronson. But I must get him out of my mind. I can't go through the rest of my life thinking of my past.* Annie finished dressing and went down the steps to start a whole new life.

As Annie approached the kitchen she could see her mother bustling around.

"Good morning, Mama," she said as she entered the kitchen. "I thought I smelled those good pancakes you always made."

"Why, yes, Annie. I thought you might need something that would stick to your ribs. You certainly have lost a lot of weight in such a short time. I will have to feed you well to put a little meat on that body of yours. My, I don't think I have ever seen anyone lose so much weight in such a short time. I will have to work hard to fatten you up a bit."

"That won't take long, Mama. You know how much I have always loved to eat."

"You might as well start now. Try these, and see if they still taste as good as they used to," Annie's mother said.

"I'm sure they do, Mama. Thank you for making my favorite breakfast. I have always loved your famous pancakes," replied Annie. "I can almost taste them already."

"After breakfast, we will get ourselves busy and see how much canning we can get done today. The garden surely had a good yield this year. Today our beans, peas, and some of our tomatoes are ready to be put up. This will keep us a little more then busy today," her mother remarked as she hastily started to clear the dishes from the table. "Take your time eating, Annie. I'm just going to get a head start on some of these vegetables."

"That sounds good to me, Mama," Annie replied. "This will be a welcome change. I'm anxious to get started. I haven't had a chance to do any work of this kind for awhile. I hope I will be of some help to you and not a hindrance."

"I'm sure you will be much more help than you can imagine. When canning, I can use all the hands I can get. You will wish you had stayed away a mite longer by the time this day is over," Annie's mother said, laughing as she went about her work. Annie knew her mother was trying to put a little happiness into her life.

Chapter 3

It took a few days for Annie to get settled again. With her strong determination and the frightening months of being married to Bronson behind her, she was anxious to overcome her past experience and fears.

To help her move on, she did small chores and ran errands for her mother. As time passed she began to feel more like her old self. She felt free and found herself smiling a little. When most of her fear had gone, she began to venture out again by going for long walks. Annie was not one to sit around, so each day it became easier for her to get on with her life. The weeks went by so fast, it was hard to believe they had turned into months.

Annie's mother decided not to waste any more time. She and Annie knew it was time to get things settled once and for all where Bronson was concerned. As soon as was possible her mother had their marriage annulled. Bronson's cruelty to Annie for the two short months they were married was unbearable.

"No one could live like that Annie. I wish I had known he was treating you so mean. I would have tried to get you away from him sooner," Annie's mother told her.

"That is in the past, Mama. With our marriage annulled, he won't hurt me anymore. And, Mama, I can go to church again."

"You are right, he is out of your life for good. Annie, you are only fifteen. You have a whole life ahead of you. This was the best way for us to handle this problem once and for all. Now you are free again."

Annie's father was very concerned about Annie. He tried to decide what he could do to help get her life in order again.

After hearing stories about the beautiful Ohio Valley being told over and over again, he decided to pack up his family and move there. He thought the change would be good for them all, and especially for Annie. As they neared the valley the view was breathtaking. Such lush green grass, tall trees, hills, valleys, and streams. He knew he had made the right choice and felt strongly that the move would be good for them all. He opened a harness shop and started hauling vegetables in this small town of Colerain. People were so friendly; they would yell a cheery hello and wave when passing.

"Mama, I am happy to be here away from Bronson. Maybe I can forget him now. Every time I think of Bronson, I break out into a sweat and feel weak all over again."

Annie's sister, Elda, overheard Annie's remark about getting weak. "Annie, for heavens sake, don't sit around thinking of what Bronson did. You said you were going to get on with your life, so get on with it! I told you about Howard. He has asked about you so often. He saw you when he was going to town for supplies and was introduced to you at a party once. He is stopping by. I want you to be here. You will like him. You are probably the prettiest girl in the whole valley, and I know he will like you, so be nice to him. That is all I ask."

"Oh Elda. Why did you invite him to come here? I'm not ready to meet anyone new yet."

"You don't have to go out with him, but the least you can do is treat him nice when he gets here."

"I'll try, but don't expect too much. It's much too soon yet, and I don't feel comfortable about meeting anyone now."

Howard arrived. He was full of anticipation at the thought of meeting Annie. Her beauty overwhelmed him. He, like others, had a hard time to keep from staring at her.

His staring made her feel uncomfortable. She tried ever so hard to be really nice, because she didn't want to make anyone feel bad. Annie visited with him for what seemed an eternity to her. Suddenly she said, "I have some work that has to be taken care of. I'm glad I met you, Howard. It was nice of you to stop by." Annie excused herself as she turned to go to her room.

"Perhaps I will see you again sometime, Annie," Howard said quickly.

"Yes, I'm sure you will," Annie replied, "since you don't live too far from here."

"I live only a few mile down the Martins Ferry Pike, so I'm sure I will see you when passing by. Goodbye for now, Annie."

"Goodbye Howard," Annie said as she walked away.

One afternoon, while she was out for a walk, deep in thought about what had happened to her, she realized she had walked much farther than usual. The sun was sinking

The Love of Annie

in the west and darkness was beginning to close in around her. She tried to quicken her steps, but she became very tired. She decided to rest, so she sat down beside a big oak tree before going back home. No sooner had she sat down than she heard a noise. Someone was coming. Her first thought was to sit quietly, so as not to be seen. She soon realized, however, that whoever it was would surely see her, no matter how quiet she was.

As Howard came closer he called out to her. "Is there some thing wrong? Are you ill?"

"No," Annie said. "I was out for a walk, and before I realized how far I had gone, the sun was setting. I decided to rest a bit before going back."

"I am going into town. You could ride along, if you would like. The ride will rest you, and I will have you home before dark."

For a minute, remembering all too vividly her past experience, she hesitated.

"I'm Howard. Do you remember me? Your sister Elda introduced us some time ago. I live just a short ways from here. Perhaps you have forgotten. It has been awhile since that day we met. If I must say so, you look a little more than just tired. Here, I will help you. I have seen you many times in the garden as I passed by your home. That's quite a walk. Please get in."

"All right," she said. "I am much more tired than I realized. My name is Annie, as you probably already know, since you remember meeting me before. I am sorry I did not recognize you. Perhaps knowing it was getting late I was a little on the apprehensive side. Howard, it is good to see you again. I must say I am truly glad to have a ride home. I am really tired."

"And it is good to see you again, Annie," Howard answered.

As they rode along Annie was surprised to find Howard to be a very nice person. It dawned on her that she was enjoying his company more than she had anticipated. All too soon, they were home.

"Thank you for the ride home, Howard. I appreciate it," Annie said as she turned to walk away.

"I'm glad you decided to let me give you a lift home. Now I will be going. Perhaps I will see you again sometime when I am on my way to town to get more supplies." He waved goodbye and went on his way.

Annie told her mother what had happened, since it was later than usual when she got home. But she did not mention how nice she thought Howard was. Nor did she say how refreshing it was to talk to someone different for a change.

From then on, if she were outside when Howard passed by, he would stop and talk for awhile before going on with his errand.

One day, Howard asked Annie to go with him to a dance. She refused, but as time went on, Howard became more persistent. Annie, still a little fearful that she would make the same tragic mistake she had made with Bronson, declined his invitations. Her only excuse was that she had too much to do each time he asked her for a date.

Howard thought she must have other friends and was trying to be nice by saying she was so busy. He decided that if this was the case, he would not stop by quite so often.

After several months had gone by, Howard again stopped when he saw Annie outside.

The Love of Annie

"Annie, there is a cakewalk at the KP Hall. I would like to go, and I would like you to be my partner. Would you be interested in going with me?"

"That would be fun, Howard. I haven't been to a cakewalk for a long time." *I'll go with him once—just once,* she thought to herself.

"The cakewalk starts at 7:30. I will pick you up at 7:15, if that is not too early for you," Howard said.

"No, that will be fine, Howard. That sounds about right. I will be ready."

"Well, now that we have that settled, I will be going. I'll see you Friday, and don't you dare change your mind," Howard remarked. As he rode out of the yard his thoughts were only on how happy he was that she had accepted his invitation at last.

Howard arrived at exactly 7:15, as he had promised. The evening proved to be just what Annie needed to relax and to laugh again.

When she got home, she was tired, so she decided to go straight to bed. As she went to her room she saw herself in the mirror. To her surprise, she seemed to have a glow that had not been there for a long time.

Howard began showing up more often. They would go for walks, then sit and talk for hours. They always had plenty to talk about.

Annie's mother, trying to protect her, questioned Annie about the frequent outings with Howard.

"Annie, you are still young. Why are you letting Howard come by so often? There is plenty of time for that. You know you have a whole life ahead of you. I think you should space his visits a little further apart."

"Mama, he is such a nice gentleman, and I really enjoy his company," she answered. "It is nothing serious, Mama. It is so nice to have someone to talk to. Someone to share in a conversation of the day's events."

Realizing the fear her mother had that she might make another mistake, she began to think she should not see Howard quite so often.

Annie always thought of other people's feelings before her own. She never wanted to cause anyone pain or trouble. Being such a young girl who had already been through so much, made her even more thoughtful of others. Her thoughts began to run rampant. She planned to tell Howard she would not see him for sometime, or perhaps not at all, thinking her mother would perhaps accept Howard if she was not too hasty with their relationship. Besides, it would give her time to get herself together.

The very sight of Howard excited Annie. Since he was so kind, so caring, and polite, she could not bring herself to tell him that she thought it was best for them to not see each other for awhile. At least not until she could convince her mother what a nice person he was.

She would wait every evening until the sun had set, then walk along the lonely road to the spot where Howard would be waiting for her. When Annie came into sight, Howard ran to meet her. He would get short of breath, and his heart would pound so fast at the sight of his Annie coming down the road.

As they embraced no words were needed. Both felt the excitement of being together. The evenings passed ever so quickly. After holding Annie in his arms so tenderly, he would gently kiss her goodbye. He knew they would meet again soon. As Annie walked away Howard would stand very still, longing to run after her.

When she got home she slipped into bed, her heart thumping like a raging river. Not wanting to hurt her mother by meeting Howard secretly, yet still feeling the need to be with him, weighed heavily on her mind. Each night after meeting Howard, she would lay in bed, thinking of the day when they would be married and be together forever.

Chapter 4

As time went on Annie began to fear that her mother was beginning to get suspicious of her many evening walks. She knew her mother was skeptical with good reason, knowing that Annie was lonely and needed a little change of pace in her otherwise dull existence.

Her mother did not know that Annie had been meeting Howard secretly. It made her feel uncomfortable and sad to know she was deceiving her. Yet, she could not wait until she could see him for a few minutes again.

One evening, as Annie ran into her lover's arms, she began to cry. Howard, filled with such anticipation of their meeting, knew Annie's sadness could mean only one thing: Their secret meetings may have to end.

"Annie," he said. "I love you. Oh how I love you, Annie. We must find a way. We must find a way before it is too late."

He kissed her ever so tenderly. Their emotions were so strong, they knew they could not wait any longer. Both realized their love for each other was so intense, and their feelings were too strong to hold back. Each admitted they had to either get married or not see each other for awhile.

Howard and Annie agreed to put their romance on hold until they could convince Annie's mother that Howard was a good, hard-working man and a wonderful person. He was a farmer by trade. But Annie's mother wanted her to marry a more sophisticated man, rather than a coal miner or a farmer.

Annie also wanted to erase any doubt she would be doing the wrong thing. So after discussing their future, and staying much longer than usual, they agreed to give themselves a little more time.

They decided not to see each other for awhile. Annie knew her love was very deep for Howard, but she did not want to make the same mistake she had made before, no matter how much she cared for him. Both felt sad, putting their courtship on hold, but they knew it to be the best way to handle this situation, at least for the time being. They cared too much for each other to take a chance, and they both knew waiting a little longer would be the right thing to do. Annie kept telling herself, *I'm only seventeen years old and there is plenty of time. Howard will understand. He will surely understand. He knows how much I care for him, and one day, we will be together again.* But her thoughts raced back to reality and her deep love for him.

As Howard held her close both tried to hold back their tears. Annie whispered, "I love you. How I love you. But we must not be too hasty. One day, Howard, we will be together. Please understand. It will not be long. I promise you, it will not be long."

Tears and emotions began to overcome him. He knew his love for Annie would never die. "I'll wait for you. I promise I will wait for you. There will never be anyone but you, Annie. I care for you so much. I love you so, so much."

"I know. I know, and I will never forget you. We will be together again." They embraced and clung to each other for some time, neither of them wanting it to end this way.

As Howard looked into Annie's beautiful, hurting eyes he bent down, lifted her chin, and kissed her ever so gently. He turned and quickly walked away. Tears burning his eyes, he didn't dare look back. He knew he would run back to his Annie if he did, and that would make her hurt even more.

Annie, feeling sad and numb, stood ever so still. She could not move. Her body began to tremble. She longed for him to come back, to touch her. *Just hold me one more time. Just one more time*, she thought.

She stood motionless as she watched Howard walk out of sight, and out of her life. "For how long?" she cried. "How long?" After she watched Howard until she could not see him any more, she slowly started back to her home. The walk seemed endless. At times she felt she should sit and rest again, but she decided to keep going. As she slowly walked home her mind was a total blank. She tried to shut out the pain of breaking up with Howard.

Fatigue took over as Annie got closer to her home. Her love for Howard weighing heavily on her heart, she opened the door and went straight to her room. Annie lay on her bed and cried until she was too exhausted to cry any more. Her hope of being with Howard again was overwhelming. But she feared that time might change things in some way that would keep them apart forever. This thought was too painful for her to bear, so she tried desperately to put it out of her mind.

~≫ The Love of Annie

After a restless night, she got up early and dressed, then went to the kitchen. Her mother had coffee ready, and she knew at a glance, something was wrong with Annie.

"What is wrong, Annie?" she asked.

"Mama, I saw Howard. I have been seeing him often."

"You have been seeing Howard! Just how long has this been going on, Annie? Why did you wait so long to tell me?"

"Please don't be angry, Mama. I've been seeing him regularly when I went for my evening walks. We realized we were beginning to care too much for each other, so I decided to quit seeing him. I didn't want to hurt you, Mama. Each night I planned to tell him, but I could not bring myself to do it. I think I love him."

"Love him? No, no, child. You are only attracted to him. It will pass. Often young girls imagine themselves in love, only to later find it was only an infatuation. Now listen to me, Annie. Put him out of your mind. You must tell him immediately that you will not see him again."

"I did tell him, Mama. I told him last night. I didn't want to hurt you, so last night we decided not to see each other for some time. But Mama, I miss him already."

"How did he take it? What did he say when you told him you would not be seeing him again?"

"I . . . didn't tell him that exactly. I told Howard we should not be in too big of a hurry, and we will get back together before long."

"Well, how did he respond to that?"

"He felt really bad, but he loves me, so he agreed we should wait just a while. He wants me to be happy, and, Mama, I love him. I do love him. He is such a tenderhearted man. I wish . . . oh, I wish you could know him as I do."

"Maybe I don't know him as well as you do, but there is time for that. It's better that you don't rush into it. Annie, I think that was the right thing to do. Give yourself more time, then someday when you are more ready to settle down, perhaps it will all fall into place."

"Fall into place, Mama? I love him so. What if Howard forgets me? Oh Mama, how I love him. He is so kind and gentle. There will never be anyone to take his place."

"Time will soften the hurt. For now, we will busy ourselves. Keeping busy helps to forget. This time of the year, cleaning, canning, and just getting ready for the cold months ahead, will help you to forget him. Time has a way of helping to mend things."

"Yes, Mama, I know. But time and work will never make me forget him. Howard is different. He is so different than anyone I have ever met. He puts everyone else first. There is not one selfish thing about him. He is a completely different type of person from Bronson. I will never find another man so unselfish and caring as Howard. Howard is a good person and most of all, he is so honest, and he reminds me of my brother Guy in so many ways. I know hard work and time are the essence of life, and it does help to heal people. But Howard is really not like most men we know."

Not wanting to antagonize her mother any more than she had already, Annie said silently, *I know I'll never forget him, and I'm sure you would like him if you would let yourself get to know him.* "Will you please give him a chance if he should ever come back?" Annie asked her mother, waiting anxiously for her response. "I pray everyday that you will like Howard. He is really nice."

The Love of Annie

"The discussion is closed right now. We have so much work ahead of us, we have to get started if we ever expect to get it all done."

Chapter 5

Days seemed to go ever so slowly. Each night when the sun was setting, Annie felt the urge to go for her walk. But she knew if she did, it would make her feel that much more lonely. So she worked harder, did a lot of reading, and tried to master learning to play the organ to keep busy. Annie had an ear for music, and her mother was a good teacher. She helped Annie daily to master her newly found interest. Annie began helping her friends to learn a few notes and teaching a little to others who were interested.

Days turned into weeks and weeks into months. Annie became sad and depressed. She did not want to be around anyone. She was irritable, stayed in her room, and seldom came down for dinner.

One day her mother noticed she had been crying. "Annie, why don't you go for a walk? You are staying to yourself far too much."

~≫ The Love of Annie

Annie could not bring herself to go for a walk. Her thoughts were always on Howard. She knew that she must keep her promise and not see him for some time, for if she did see him, there would be no turning away from him again. *We must give ourselves just a little more time,* she thought. *Then perhaps Mama will realize how good he is and not judge him so harshly.*

Annie wondered how long it would be, or if she ever would see him again. Tears were always near the surface. At the mere mention of his name she would cry. No matter how hard she tried not to, she could not hold back the tears. Often she would find herself wondering if Howard missed her and if he felt the same agonizing loneliness that she was feeling for him. *Yes, he is as lonely as I am, I'm sure. Our love for each other is so deep. Poor, poor Howard,* she thought. *He is so kind and patient. I know he misses me and is as lonely as I am. How I wish I could see him again.*

Howard was also so sad that every evening he'd go to their meeting place by the big oak tree and the whistling pines. He would sit alone; waiting and hoping that his Annie just might miss him also, miss him enough to come there, too.

Annie's mother kept a close eye on her. She knew every move she made and kept her busy with her music. Anything to keep her from trying to see Howard. Her mother was so against them being together. She wanted her to marry someone else, not a coal miner or farmer. No one really seemed good enough for Annie, according to her mother.

After months and months passed without seeing his Annie, Howard turned to working long hours. His heart broken and his hopes and dreams all gone, he worked hard to try to get over her. But this was to no avail. He kept waiting and waiting to hear from her.

One night, frail and broken-hearted, Annie knew her mother had come down with symptoms of a cold and gone to bed early. Overcome with a longing to see Howard, she slipped out of the house and hurried as fast as she could, hoping by chance Howard would be there at their old meeting place. Out of breath, she finally reached her destination amongst the beautiful whistling pines. Howard was not there. So much time had gone by with no Annie that he had given in to his grief and worked hard to keep from completely losing himself. Yet he hoped one day to see her again, and he vowed he would never give up the thought of being with her, no matter how long it took him. Often Howard felt his prayers were not being heard.

Annie waited, watching every moving leaf, thinking it was the sound of Howard coming. She became more stricken with grief when she realized that it was not Howard and that he would not be coming. She felt depressed. After what seemed like forever, waiting and hoping that maybe, just maybe, Howard would be there and they would follow through with their plans to be married, she thought she had better get on her way. *Howard had no way of knowing I would be here, so of course he would not come,* she thought. She took one last look around her to be sure he was not coming before starting back home.

Her eyes swollen and red from crying, and her body tired and trembling with disappointment, she started the long walk back home.

She went straight to her room and climbed slowly into bed, hoping that her mother had not heard her come in. After some time, Annie finally drifted off to sleep, not knowing that Howard, too, had been desperately lonely for her this night, the same night that Annie had gone looking for him. He, too, decided he would go to their meeting place by the old oak tree and the beautiful pines. Neither knew the other one had been there.

As time went on Annie became so disheartened and lonely because she could not see Howard. She made quilts, studied her music daily, and lived a quiet life. Time passed by ever so slowly. There didn't seem to be anything that could make her forget the times she had spent with Howard. The more she tried to put him out of her mind, the more she seemed to miss him. But she knew she had to go on if she wanted to keep alive her hopes of seeing and being with him again.

Annie tried with all of her being to please her mother, although she was old enough to do things on her own. Her past experiences with Bronson had taught her a lot about life. She felt that by her living at home, maybe someday her mother would see the good in Howard, and she would be more willing to accept him.

Chapter 6

Annie was close to her father. She loved and admired him very much. He loved her also, and it grieved him to see her so brokenhearted and lonely. He took Annie on long rides every evening to put a little joy in her life or to at least break the monotony of another dull day.

Annie's father would hitch up the horse and buggy, and the two of them would ride along the country roads. It was so pretty, almost breathtaking with the deep shades of green-colored leaves, just around every bend in the road and then another hill laden with wild flowers. "The hills and valleys of Ohio are always a sight to behold when the sun begins to disappear," Annie would tell her father. "It's a sight one could never forget, no matter how hard they tried." The winter months were also pretty, although their rides were not as often because of the cold. The snow-covered hills were also something to remember.

Her father wanted to help Annie get through this depression. He was aware of her mother's feelings about Annie seeing Howard again. He knew he'd have an argument if he tried to interfere with whatever her plans for their daughter happened to be.

After talking and listening to Annie's heartbreak, he would pat Annie's hand and tell her, "Someday, little girl, someday . . . Yes, yes, someday your dreams will come true. I promise you. Yes, honey, they will come true."

She knew her father was only trying to comfort her, but she loved him for trying. Annie realized he would never win an argument with her mother, no matter how hard he tried, and tomorrow would end up being the same as today.

Annie's brother, Guy, was also very fond of his sister, and he, too, worried about her unhappiness. Often he would appear at her room door and the two of them would sit for hours at a time just talking. He was constantly trying to comfort his favorite sister.

When Guy was about to enter the teen years, on occasion, he became a little belligerent if things didn't go his way. This would really make his mother angry. She would lock him in his room so that no one would see how badly he was behaving. When this happened, it hurt Annie very much. She felt it was so degrading and humiliating. It drew Annie and Guy closer to each other, however, and Annie would often sneak into his room to cheer him up as he had done when she was punished in the past. Guy was reserved and kind, a very caring person. He would get upset when he knew Annie was getting a raw deal. Since Guy and Annie both felt their mother's rejection, they found their relationship grew even stronger. Although they loved their sisters, Elda and Edna, they had a very strong bond between the two of them that the others did not have. Guy tried to protect Annie from more hurt or pain every chance he had. He was continually trying to lift Annie's spirits.

One day, when dinner was over and the household chores were done, Annie was waiting for Guy to come home. When he did not come as quickly as she thought he would, she went out to the garden. She was anxious for her brother to come home so they could talk. Suddenly, she heard some one calling her name. Her uncle was standing close behind her. He had come from the State of Virginia with a young man whom Annie's father had sent for, to help in his harness shop.

As she turned to speak to her uncle she noticed a striking gentleman with him. "Annie, this is Carper McPeak. Carper is going to stay for awhile and help in the harness shop. Your father sent for him because he needed help. Carper was looking for a job. He felt he could help your father also with his hauling of vegetables and so on."

"I'm glad to meet you," Annie said. "Please come in. Mama will be happy to know you are here."

While they were getting acquainted with their new guest, Guy came home. He immediately took a liking to Carper. They seemed to have a lot to talk about, so Annie and her mother went to prepare supper while the men got to know each other better. After they had eaten, Guy showed Carper to the bedroom they would be sharing.

Carper was a hard worker, and a fun-loving kind man. He and Guy became very good friends. They spent all of their free time together. As time passed they began to include Annie in some of their outings. They knew Annie was a very lonely girl these days. They didn't want her to know they asked her to go along because they felt sorry for her. Teasing her, they told her they brought her along to protect them from other women, or sometimes they would tell her she could fight off the wolves, if they happened to meet up with one. Annie loved their joking and usually she would answer quickly, "Don't worry, I know I can handle the situation. Just keep going."

The family grew very fond of Carper—he seemed to fit right in. He helped around the house doing odd jobs, anything to show his appreciation of being there, for he loved his job in the harness shop.

As time went on Guy, Carper, and Annie sat together in the evenings, joking and talking. Mostly, Guy and Carper tried putting a little joy into Annie's life. They wanted so badly to help her to be happy again.

As Carper was working in the shop one day, thinking of what he would do that evening, he thought about Annie. He began to realize his feelings for her were more than for a friend in a crisis. To his surprise, he found himself wanting to be alone with her. In the previous months, they'd had a sister-and-brother relationship. He was someone to talk to when she needed a good listener, someone who understood how she felt, and cared enough to let her say what was bothering her.

As the months passed Carper became very fond of Annie. One day, while he was talking to Guy, Carper confided to his friend that Annie was beginning to mean more to him than a friend. "Would you mind if I would ask her to go riding with me? Perhaps she will not want to go, but I would like to ask her. We are friends, Guy, and your family means a lot to me. Letting me live here with you has meant so much. It is nice to be close to where my work is and not have to get up so early. Also, I have the conveniences of home.

"I would treat Annie right. If you think I should not intrude upon her personal life, I won't. You may be young, Guy, but you are sensitive, and you love Annie and care for her happiness as I do."

"Yes. Yes, Carper, I wish you would ask Annie out. She has been home so long it might be good for her. Perhaps this may be what she needs to lift her out of this deep depression. Goodness knows anything to help her to find a little peace in her life would be nice. Do you know, Carper, I get a little disturbed when I think of how Annie felt when she had to marry Bronson just to please someone else. Being young and foolish is one thing, but it's not right to be pressured into something you are not sure you want at such a young age. I know other people seem to pawn their children off to be married, but somehow, it seems to me, you should be able to marry someone you have selected yourself. But what do I know? Huh! Not much I guess, or I would know the answers to questions like that. Anyway, I am happy you care for Annie. She will probably think you are feeling sorry for her, but I know differently. Carper, as much as I hate to tell you this, you do have a way about you that seems to add a little something extra to my days also. I don't want to inflate that ego of yours, but I have to admit it is nice to have you around. I really don't want you to get a big head, so forget what I said."

"Oh!" Carper replied. "I add something to your day all right, probably a headache."

"I wouldn't say that, Carper. I was thinking more along the line of an anxiety attack," Guy answered quickly.

"Wow! You are sure on the ball today! I think I'll get back to work while I'm still ahead," replied Carper. "I will see what happens when I see Annie later on this evening.

The Love of Annie

Thanks for agreeing that my asking her to go for a ride tonight might be the thing to do. You have to admit, at least, I do have some good traits," Carper quipped.

"Yes, I'm sure you do, I just haven't seen them yet," Guy said.

"Get out of here! I'm not getting paid to listen to you," Carper answered.

"OK, OK, I'm going, and I do hope Annie will agree to at least go for a ride with you. See you later! Let me know what Annie's answer is when you ask her to go with you," Guy said as he turned to leave.

" OK," Carper hollered as Guy went on his way.

Chapter 7

That evening after dinner was over and the dishes were done, Carper said casually, "Annie, how about you and I going for a little drive? It's too lovely of an evening to be in the house."

Immediately, Annie refused. "I am not quite ready to start another friendship this soon." *Besides, Howard is still so much on my mind,* she thought to herself. *I felt secure when I was with Howard. Although fear is still too close to the surface because of Bronson's cruelty, as well as the deep reservations that still haunt me, Howard had a way of making me feel secure. But, then, Howard is different. His kind gentle ways, sincerity, honesty, and being such a humble man, everyone trusts him. No one can ever take Howard's place in my life. How I miss him at times.*

Annie often walked to the little church the family attended. As she walked the distance she would pray for God to help her to get through another day. Annie was taught that praying is the answer to all problems. *And prayer has gotten me through each day so far*, she thought as she neared the church. *The sermon makes me feel a little more lighthearted when I feel blue.*

One day, while Annie was sitting alone in the swing on the porch, Carper quietly sat down beside her. Neither said anything for a long time. Carper reached over and put his hand on Annie's. "I'll give you a penny for your thoughts."

"You would get gypped. They aren't worth too much," she quipped.

"I know how you feel, Annie, but you must get on with your life. Please let me help. You are a lovely lady, and it saddens me to watch you be sad day after day after day. It is almost as though you dread facing each day or even getting up in the morning. Let me help you. Let me help you, Annie. Please?"

"What can anyone do, Carper?" she asked.

"Well, for a start, we might discuss it over a cup of tea." Smiling a little, Annie went into the kitchen, made each of them a cup of tea, and brought it back to the swing.

"Well, this is a start. We will take it from here. We will lick this thing. No one, not even Bronson, is going to ruin your life. He was a scoundrel, Annie. I can't believe anyone being that selfish, only wanting to satisfy his own needs. Please, Annie, just give me a chance. I know we can get you over this culprit and what he did to you."

After sitting and talking the evening away, both decided they had talked long enough. "We are overly tired tonight, Annie, so I suggest that we call it a night, and we will get a good rest before worrying about our problems we have to face tomorrow."

When she went to her room, Annie didn't know what Carper's intentions were, but she was too exhausted to care.

Since Carper shared a room with Guy, he was exceptionally quiet, so he would not wake Guy as he climbed into bed. He lay for hours trying to think of the best way to help Annie.

Carper and Annie began spending more time just talking and laughing together. It helped time to pass a little more smoothly for Annie.

Her mother was pleased to hear her daughter laugh again. Some of her hopeless feelings had disappeared.

Carper and Guy confided to each other that maybe enough time had lapsed, and Annie might be ready to start her life in a different direction. It's worth trying again anyway, they decided.

One day as Annie was in the garden watering the flowers someone gently touched her on the shoulder, and said, "You are as pretty as any flower in your garden." She turned around and saw it was Carper.

"You must say that to every girl."

"Oh, no," he said. "Only to the ones I see watering flowers." Knowing he was kidding her, she began to laugh.

"Annie, now don't say no. Let's go for that ride tonight. It is a beautiful night."

"All right. You won't give up, so just give me a little time to change my clothes. I'll be ready in a few minutes. Now don't you get any ideas about changing your mind, just because I said I would go," Annie remarked as she hastily left the garden.

"Huh!" he yelled. "Not a chance you are going to be that lucky. Just be quick. It's pretty out, just before the sun goes down."

As they rode along she thought, *This is refreshing. It does feel good to be doing something again.*

~≫ The Love of Annie

The evening passed by more quickly than she expected. Upon arriving home, Carper announced, "We will do this again. I hope you enjoyed the ride, Annie."

"I did, Carper. It was very nice, thank you."

Their outings became more frequent. Guy teasingly remarked, "Isn't it funny how quickly one forgets his best friend when there is a lady involved?"

"It is indeed," replied Carper, "and weren't you taught two is company and three is a crowd?"

"Oh, yes indeed. Ah yes, I get the picture. Well, I have a few things of my own to take care of. See you later."

Each day Annie found herself enjoying Carper's company a little more. They went for long walks and rode through tree-lined country roads. Often Guy would ride along to have something to do or because they wanted his company.

Annie was forever thinking back to what her marriage with Bronson was like. She remembered the suffering and disappointment in herself and the long nights of hurting from his pinching and biting. This made her hold back her feelings and not tell anyone how she felt. This fear kept her from enjoying Carper's company. She was apprehensive and a little fearful of someone new in her life. The thought of making another mistake was constantly on her mind.

At night she would find herself lying awake, trying to decide if she should quit going out with Carper, or if going with him was better than sitting around as most people do, when they have nothing else of real interest to keep them occupied.

Remembering how lonely she had been before she began going out with Carper helped her to go to sleep. She weighed her thoughts back and forth, trying to decide what was the better thing for her to do. She would remind herself that Carper was really good to her, and that she was a little more at peace with herself now than before she went with him. Being with Carper helped to take her mind off of how much she missed Howard and the cruelty Bronson had inflicted upon her. After she lay quietly for some time, she would eventually drift off to sleep.

Carper decided he would not try to see Annie any more than at meal time or maybe when passing in the halls or working in the garden. This was too much for him seeing Annie so sad. It was more than he could cope with. It was definitely more than he could handle. He awoke one morning feeling so upset at not being able to be with her, he decided he should find another job, so as not to add to Annie's unhappiness.

As the day passed Carper decided to ask Annie to go for a ride with him after supper. He thought that maybe he could find out why she was avoiding him.

When Annie finally came down for supper, she hardly seemed to notice that Carper was around. After supper was over and the dishes done, she went back to her room without so much as a word to Carper.

Feeling so down, he decided perhaps he should leave and find a job somewhere else even sooner then he had planned. Then Annie would not feel herself being pushed into a relationship she was not ready for. This, he knew, would be hard for him to do with jobs being scarce and knowing he would miss her so much. Not seeing her would be almost unbearable. *I must think this through before it's too late,* he thought.

He went to bed early to make his decision. Alone in his room the evening seemed even longer. With Guy being out later than usual, it gave Carper time to think. Thinking it

～ The Love of Annie

best for everyone, he decided to tell Annie he was leaving. But not until the next day, after his day's work was finished and supper was over.

While working all day the thought of leaving was almost too much for him. Being such a kind person, he made his decision. Thinking Annie did not care for him, he decided he would not stand in her way any longer. Carper prayed that Annie would change her mind, but he felt hopeless at this time.

After supper, he calmly announced he would be leaving early the next day to find work elsewhere. To Annie's surprise, the thought of not having him around distressed her. "Carper, please don't leave. Daddy needs you here. If you leave, Daddy will have no one to help in the shop, and then . . . then we will miss you. Our home will seem so empty. It has been well over a year now since you came here. Where would you go?"

After a deep sigh, Carper looked at Annie, almost as if it was too much for him to understand. He went back to the shop, trying to think what Annie's outburst was all about, and his hopes began to rise again.

When he came in much later, Annie was waiting for him. "Carper, Carper. It's such a nice night. I really would like to go for a walk. You have asked me so many times, but I was frightened. Sometimes I wake in the night and relive what it was like when I was with Bronson. My head is wet with perspiration, and I'm shaking. Then I realize it was only a nightmare. Please understand, Carper. It was not you I was hiding from. I guess . . . I guess I'm trying to hide from myself, from my own feelings. Fear has a way of taking over my life. When you said you were leaving, it . . . it . . . Carper, it made me want you to stay. Please don't go away, Carper."

"Annie, you must know by now that I care for you. Yes, I really care for you. Each day I seem to care for you more. Do you really want me to stay? You wouldn't say that if you didn't want me here, would you?"

"No, no, Carper. You have kept me from falling to pieces. I need someone. I need you. Please stay. Please stay, at least for a little while longer."

The two of them walked out into the night, trying hard to understand this sudden change of events. Carper said, "Annie, Annie. I didn't think you would ever say you needed me. And I need you." For the first time, he drew her close and gently pecked her with a kiss on her forehead.

As they walked back to the house both felt more light-hearted and so much happier than before. They decided not to tell anyone about this evening, at least not until later.

The next morning at breakfast, Annie, with the innocence of a child, announced that Carper wanted to keep his job at the shop, and he wanted to continue helping with the hauling of vegetables.

"Really! You plan staying on here, Carper?" Annie's father asked.

"Yes. I decided if you will still be needing my help, I would like to stay. You have a very persuasive daughter."

With a gleam in his eye, her father got up from the table and patted Annie on her shoulder, then went to the shop with Carper immediately following. Annie's father was very fond of Carper and was very pleased they were spending more time together again.

"Carper, I can't help but notice. Annie and you are spending more evenings together. Annie has been through so much already, I could not bear to see her suffer any more."

~≼ The Love of Annie

"I have become very fond of her, sir. I could never hurt her," Carper replied. "That's the reason I planned to leave. I felt my being here was perhaps making her unhappy. But now Annie seems to really want me to stay, and I want what is best for her, sir. I love her, and I know she would make me happy. But I must make sure this is what she wants also."

"This is what I have hoped for, Carper. Someone to care for her. Someone to help her find some happiness again. Carper, if you can make Annie happy, that is what I want for her. I wish the very best for you. I'll rest much better knowing you love her and will take care of her. She wants to please everyone far too much, Carper."

"Yes, I know," he replied. "We plan being together tonight. Now I had better get back to work. I at least want to earn my supper."

"Carper, your loving and caring for Annie has done so much more than just earning your supper. Thank you, son. Thank you for being here. Now I guess we had better finish this job. Supper will be ready soon, and I'm sure you know how women are when they are ready to eat. They want to get it over with. I guess we had better get moving. We would hate to get their dander up. Besides, my stomach is rubbing against my backbone, I'm so hungry," Annie's father replied, with a twinkle in his eye.

The thought of Carper being there for Annie and to add a little happiness to her life was all that mattered to Annie's father. He loved Carper for caring for Annie so much.

Chapter 8

Annie, thinking of her feelings for Carper and not seeing Howard for so long, decided to get on with her life. "I'll probably never see Howard again, sad as it is, but life goes on, and so must I. By now, he's probably met someone and has his own family. I hope he is happy. He deserves to be happy. No one knows how much I'd like to see him once more."

The next time Carper and Annie were alone, they went for a ride. While riding along the tree-lined country road, they noticed the sheer beauty in the early evening. The sun was just sinking below the hills and the lush green grass greeted them on every little knoll and bend in the road. "With so many lilacs and wild flowers growing all around, the smell of the evening breeze is almost enough to take your breath away," Annie remarked.

"Yes, both roses and lilacs have such a sweet smell," replied Carper.

Not wanting to miss any of the scenery, they rode farther than they had planned, just taking in the beauty of the valley and breathing in the fresh air. "Isn't this exhilarating, this fresh air and the lovely fragrance from the flowers? The smell of lilacs and wild roses seem to float through the air. I'm happy people plant lilacs. I love their sweet smell. The different fragrances blend in together," Annie remarked.

The sun rested for the night and the stars looked like a million diamonds, all sparkling at once. Carper could not keep his eyes off of Annie. He pulled the buggy to the side of the road, stopped abruptly, and looked down into Annie's face. "Your eyes are brighter than the brightest star in the heavens. Annie, I want you to marry me. I don't want to rush you, but you know how much I love you. Will you marry me, Annie? You don't have to tell me the answer tonight. You can think about it if you want more time."

"I have thought about it, Carper. Yes. Yes, I will marry you! You have brought me peace of mind, and I do love you, Carper. When I needed someone so badly, when I felt my life was over, you were there for me. Yes, I do love you."

"How soon shall we make our plans?" Carper queried. "Would tomorrow be too soon?" he asked jokingly, knowing that would really be rushing things.

"Not if you can wait until I wash my hair," she quipped.

Laughing at her quick wit, he drew her close and kissed her, over and over again. Both were so happy they wanted to tell their good news right away. They decided to be married very quickly the following week.

Annie's mother and dad were so pleased with the announcement and agreed the day they picked was perfect.

The week went by so fast. They had a small wedding at the church they had attended before. Only Annie's immediate family attended the ceremony. Carper's family lived in Virginia, and the distance was too far for his family to attend the wedding. They found a little house in Maynard, Ohio. Carper continued to work at the harness shop, until a relative got him a job in the coal mine. The pay was better, and with money so scarce, they needed the extra. He started his new job after giving Annie's dad a few days to find a man to replace him. In only a few week's time, they had their own little home. Carper had a job as a coal miner, and they were ready for a whole new life.

Annie was content having someone to love and to share her life. Everything seemed to fall into place. Guy lived only a short distance from Carper and Annie's home. He was always standing by to help with anything they might need. He was more than elated to see Annie finally living a peaceful life and would often drop in unexpectedly, always with a wisecrack to get Carper going. They enjoyed every word said between them.

"Carper, do you think I could get a job in the mine where you are working? You don't seem to be too apprehensive working there, and I could use a job where I can make more money."

"Well, Guy, the pay's good, but the work is very dirty. There is a lot of danger in that dark black hole in the ground. As you know Guy, men are often killed. Coal mines have cave-ins. Heaps and heaps of that black stuff can let go and bury you alive, or gas can form and suffocate you. I know you want a good job, but I don't want anything to happen to you. I would blame myself for getting you in that cold,

cold, black hole, if something should go wrong and you would get hurt."

After a while, Carper reluctantly did get Guy a job in the coal mine. Guy, too, was a very young man, as most coal miners were. Sixteen years old was often the age the young men started to work in the mines. Guy liked the extra income the coal mines paid. This job was another thing Guy and Carper had in common. They had more things of interest to talk about.

One day as Carper and Guy were talking, Annie appeared at the door looking like the cat that swallowed the canary. "Just what have you got on your mind, my dear? I've seen that look enough times, so let's have it. Why the gloating look?" Carper asked.

"Well," Annie replied, " I have always liked spending your hard-earned money, so how would you like me spending even more?"

"Huh! Well, let me see. Just how can you spend more when you have less?"

"Oh I'm sure you will find a way when you look down into a wee little baby's face and know you are the daddy."

"You . . . you mean . . . no . . . no, it can't be. Are you sure? You mean we are going to have a baby!"

"Yes, Carper. I've kept it to myself until I knew for sure."

"Oh Annie! Annie! That's great! We are going to have a baby. Come here, you lovely lady."

She lifted her head as he kissed her. He could not hide his happiness. "Did you hear that, Guy? Did you hear that? We are going to have a baby!"

"I heard it, Carper, and so did all the neighbors in the next block."

The Love of Annie

"Well, one thing, Annie. We know a good uncle who will be a dandy person to leave our new baby with if we want to run around all night. Our little boy will love you, Guy."

"On that thought, I'll make my exit," Guy said jokingly, "and leave you two lovebirds alone. See you later."

As Guy went on his way Annie remarked, "By the way, Carper, you seem so confident our baby is going to be a boy. Just how will you feel when our little one turns out to be a girl?"

"Oh, give me an hour to think about it. No, no, I don't need any time. I'm so happy, you could have six all at once, and I would be all the more happy."

"Well now don't get carried away. One at a time will be just fine with me."

"Me too," he said as he gave her another kiss on her cheek. "You know a little girl would be nice," Carper told Annie, touching her ever so tenderly on her hand.

Each day plans were made for the new arrival, and finally a little girl was born. Without any hesitation, Carper said he wanted to name her Annie Ruth. "We will call her Ruth. She is the spitting image of you, Annie."

"No wonder she is such a pretty baby," she replied.

"Well, I can't argue with that, I guess," Carper answered, smiling a little. "Just wait until our next baby comes along. It will be a boy. Then I will gloat and brag how much he looks like me. On second thought, I wouldn't want a baby to look like me. He would probably be the best-looking chump in the block, and the kids would all pick on him. We don't want that, so I will be happy if our kids can just be healthy. That's all we want. We are lucky to have such a good baby, aren't we?"

～ The Love of Annie

"Yes, she is a pretty little bundle of joy. It's hard to believe she is ours. And she is such a healthy little thing. That's really what counts."

Things went well for Carper, Annie, and their little girl. The sadness and depression was no longer a part of Annie's life. When little Ruthie, as they called her, was past two years old, Johnny was born. Life for Annie and Carper was quiet, but happy. They were content in their little home with their two little ones.

One day as Annie was attending to her two small children and preparing their supper, a knock at the door startled her. She hurriedly opened the door. Two men greeted her.

As they stepped inside the older one spoke ever so gently. "Mrs. McPeak," he said. "You are Annie McPeak?"

"Yes, I am Mrs. McPeak. Is there something wrong? Is my mother ill?"

"No . . . no, it isn't your mother. I'm so sorry to tell you, but your husband has been hurt in the coal mines."

"Hurt! Where is he? How bad is he hurt? Oh please tell me, how bad is he hurt?"

"Well, ma'am, it is serious, but he was rushed to the doctor, and we all hope he will be OK."

"I must see him. Please, can I go see him?"

"Yes, we will take you there. We will get you to the hospital as soon as you can get ready to go."

As Annie quickly dressed her face turned ashen-white. The color had drained from her pretty face from fear of how badly he might be hurt. She dressed the children quickly, so they could get to him as soon as possible.

Carper had been crushed beneath coal from a cave-in. His stomach was crushed so badly, his breath was almost gone, and they feared he would stop breathing entirely.

Carper had been rushed to a little hospital, not too far from the coal mine where he worked.

When Annie got to his side, he lay so still. As Annie held his hand she prayed, "Please God. Please God. Please don't let him die. Please don't let him die."

The good doctor said, "You had better get yourself a little rest, Annie. This could go on for hours on end. You can't let yourself get too tired. You know the two little ones need you also."

"Yes, I know, Doctor. I will rest as soon as I see how Carper is coming along."

After what seemed an eternity, Carper's eyes moved. He didn't know Annie was by his side. He closed his eyes again.

"Please, please, God. Don't let him die." Not being able to hide her fear, Annie began to cry.

Almost as if he wanted to comfort Annie, Carper slowly opened his eyes and reached for Annie's hand. He squeezed it, mustered a small smile, and then sank back into a deep sleep. Annie waited and waited, praying constantly for the danger to pass. The doctor watched over him day and night.

After several days had passed, Carper began to show signs of getting better, and in a short time he was out of the hospital and back home again.

Annie vowed she would nurse him back to health. Day after day, she did everything she could. She made broth, puddings, and anything she thought would be good for him. At last their fear was gone, and both of them relaxed. Carper grew stronger and stronger each day. Feeling he was out of danger, Annie was very happy.

At this time, little Ruthie was three years old and Johnny, nine months. "The fun age to be around," Carper and Annie remarked. They began to laugh. "A nine-month-old baby and a three year old . . . the fun age. Ha, we must be crazy," Annie said.

"I would say 'busy age,' but both are so precious," Carper replied. "It would surely be a dull home without those two, wouldn't it, Annie?"

"My, I should say so. Without the noise they make, we would have to take up some hobby to keep from getting bored," Annie continued.

"Now, I wouldn't go so far as to say that, but the house would be awfully quiet without them," Carper said, just before he dozed off to sleep.

Chapter 9

A few days had gone by when Carper became very ill. He experienced days of anguish, pain, and a high, out-of-control fever. The old family doctor said, "It looks like an infection of some sort has set in. I will give him this medicine. This is a very strong medication, and it should put a stop to the infection. I have another call to make, then I will be back to check on Carper."

When the doctor returned, Carper was even worse than when he had left. "Annie, I'm afraid peritonitis has set in. The medicine I gave him should have prevented this. I was certain it would work. Peritonitis is our greatest fear with an injury of this kind."

Carper lay day after day, his fever worsening. Annie stayed by his bedside day and night, but nothing could keep the fever from ravishing his body.

On a bad, stormy day, the wind howling through the woods and the roads blocked from the fallen trees, the doctor finally arrived again, only to find Carper lying very still.

~~ The Love of Annie

He had chills and a burning fever. Annie and her two small children were kneeling by his bedside. She was trying to comfort him with all the love and strength she had.

After long hours of doing everything the doctor could do to help him, Carper died in Annie's arms as their two little ones looked on. They were too young to realize their daddy had just died, and their lives were about to change now that their daddy was gone.

Annie went into deep despair over Carper's death. Not knowing how or what to do, she tried to raise her children alone. Her grief and loneliness proved to be too much for her, however, and she had all she could do to get through each day. Finally after much persuasion, she moved back to her parent's home. With her mother's help, she got through the heartbreak. This was a big help to Annie, since Carper and Annie had very little money when he died. By keeping busy and raising two children, time passed for her.

Annie's grief didn't seem to lessen much. Her thoughts invariably were on the few short years Carper and she had together and wondering how she could possibly get the two little ones raised without the guidance of their father.

Guy was still working in the coal mines, but he kept a watchful eye on Annie, perhaps even a closer watch over her now that Carper had died. Guy often thought of his best friend and brother-in-law who had warned him of the dangers of the coal mine. Now Guy was the one who lived to see the terrible death of his closest friend. Though his time was limited, he still found time to visit his favorite sister. Annie still meant too much to him to let her go through this alone.

Carper's death weighed heavily on his mind. More so than Guy thought it would. Working in the mines, Guy now and then felt a little frightened. Perhaps a little more so than before Carper's death.

Annie loved it when Guy would come to visit. At the young age of twenty-two, and with so much having already happened to her, she was a little frightened. She felt again the awful pain of being alone through long days and endless nights. Guy's visits helped her to get through another day, along with asking God for his help daily.

One night, after tucking the two little ones in bed, Annie decided to go for a walk, as she had done before she had married Carper. The old familiar walk didn't seem to help. She was more tired and restless, and she climbed into bed, exhausted.

Day after day, her only happiness was the visits Guy paid her, and, of course, her children. Often she thought how lucky she was to have these little ones to look after.

How she loved Guy. *He never, ever changed,* she thought. *He is the same Guy I love, and he is still protecting me now, as he did when we were children at home. He has this nice way about him, knowing just the right things to say to cheer me up.* Guy could always add a little brightness to her otherwise dull existence.

As Annie toiled day after day, trying to put aside all the unhappiness that had passed through her young life, she became very weary. She had experienced too much for a young woman in her early twenties. First, she had a husband who seemed to care for her so much, but whom then suddenly began to hurt and abuse her daily. Then she lost a wonderful husband and was left with two small children to raise. That loss seemed overwhelming.

Annie felt very helpless. It was so frightening having no place or people to turn to. *I'm glad my mother wants me to live here with them,* she thought. But with no father to help her with the children, it was a monumental task for her, and she was heartbroken at being alone again. Her strong will to make the best of her life, regardless of what fate had dealt her, kept her going, along with her faith in God.

Often Annie went for a walk in the evening after the children said their prayers and were tucked safely in bed. Walking seemed to bring back memories of years gone by. However, . . . they were memories that were lost forever. . . . memories that perhaps would never be recaptured, so she began to walk less and less. She passed the time playing with the little ones instead of going for her evening walks.

Chapter 10

Sometimes, while playing with the children in the yard, Annie found herself thinking of Howard, how deeply they had been in love and how circumstances had driven them apart. She also remembered how she had missed him so terribly and about the feeling of being alone. The long days, the hope, and the waiting, . . . yes, the waiting for a lover she had never seen again. Now so much time had passed, she was sure Howard had met someone else and settled in his own home. She put him out of her mind, thinking she would never see him again, anyway.

One day, sitting in the swing alone, she fell asleep. She was tired from working in the garden and tending to the children. She heard a sweet-sounding voice. "Annie, . . . Annie, . . ." Annie opened her eyes. As she looked up she thought she had been dreaming.

"Howard! Howard, . . . is that you?" Annie rubbed her eyes, not trusting what she saw. When she looked up again, she was looking into Howard's face. Not believing what she was seeing, she closed her eyes again. She thought that if she closed her eyes reality would set in, and she would know she had been dreaming. Annie did not want to believe it was only a dream, but it could not be happening. *I must have slept hard to dream like that,* she thought.

Suddenly, Howard reached down and gently touched her hand. "It's me, Annie. It's me. Don't be afraid. I'm here, Annie. I'm really here."

"Howard, . . . It is you. It is you. Tell me I'm . . . I'm not dreaming, am I? I . . . I must be dreaming."

"No, Annie, you are not dreaming. It is me. It's Howard. When I saw you sitting alone, I thought . . . well, I just could not go on by. I had to stop. Do you mind that I stopped, Annie? Is it OK?"

"Of course it is OK, Howard. I can't believe it is you. It has been so long, so . . . so long, Howard. I can't believe you are here. Please sit down."

"Thanks. I will sit a spell, if you are sure it is all right."

"Please do. I want to know all about you, where you've been, and all that's happened."

"We will get to me later. First I want to know how you are doing during such a critical time in your life. How are you doing, Annie? I know this has to be the worst thing that can happen to a young mother, to lose her husband and be left alone to raise two small children. Are you sure you are all right?"

"Yes, Howard. I will be fine. It will take time, but I will be all right."

"I heard about your husband dying from those injuries in the coal mines. I'm so sorry such a bad thing had to happen to you. It must have been very devastating. One day being content in your life, and the next day your whole life falls apart. I'm truly sorry, Annie. I am really sorry," Howard said, ever so softly.

"It is awful. The children are young, and they are so restless at times. They can't understand why their daddy doesn't come home anymore. Little Ruthie often asks, 'Where is Daddy?' It is sad to watch her little face. The sadness in her eyes alone shows how much she misses her daddy. She asks, 'Don't Daddy want us anymore? Don't my daddy like me and Johnny? Mommy, where is my daddy? I want to see Daddy.' It is so hard to explain to her how much he loved them, but that he had to go away."

"Give the children more time, and they will be OK," Howard said. "I'm sure with you being with them and guiding them daily, they will be fine. It will take a lot of time and patience, but you will give that along with your deep love."

"Life goes on, and I'm doing all I can to help them grow up strong and healthy. I try to keep them occupied so they can put some of the hurt and loneliness aside."

"I'm sure you are doing everything possible. There is only so much you can do. I know you are a good mother."

"We will be fine, Howard. Now tell me what you have been doing."

"Well, not a lot. I'm still living on the farm with my father."

"Then you mean you have never married? You are not married after all of these years? Howard, I thought perhaps you had found someone, someone to love and . . . and to help you find a little happiness."

"Oh, I did, a few years ago. When we parted, and as the years went by, I always knew I could never care for anyone else but you, Annie. There has never been anyone else I could find any sort of happiness with. I dated now and then, and for awhile, I was seeing a lady. But that's not important. I was happy to help my father. His health was failing, so I took over the workload for him. I kept busy every day.

"My father needed help, and I needed something to get through the days ahead, so it was good for both of us. My mother was gone, and, as I said, I did take over his workload.

"Annie, it is so nice to see you again. I've seen you and the children in the yard, and I often wanted to tell you how sorry I was to hear about Carper's death. But I wasn't sure if it was the proper thing to do under the circumstances, so I forced myself to move on."

"Howard, you are welcome to stop by any time you are on your way to town. I'm sure the children would love having someone else besides me to talk to once in awhile."

"Annie, I would love to occasionally, if you are sure it won't bother the little ones. But I certainly don't want to be a nuisance to you."

"Nonsense, Howard. I would enjoy seeing you."

"Well then, since you don't mind, I will drop in again. I'll be going now. I have a lot of work to do when I get home. It was really nice seeing you. The way those clouds are churning up there, and with the lightning becoming much sharper than before, I had better go now, before it gets any worse."

Annie could not believe this day. Happiness filled her heart as never before. Sound asleep, and awakened by Howard's loving voice. "It is truly unbelievable," she said aloud.

As she watched Howard drive away her heart began to skip a beat. Her eyes flashed almost even keel to the bright flashes of lightning streaking across the sky. As she went into the house she was humming her favorite song.

> Only as far as the porch Mama,
> I want to go out to the porch.
> It's a beautiful night, the moon's shining bright.
> I'm just going out to the porch.

"Why are you so happy, Annie?" her mother asked. "My child, I haven't seen you look this happy for months and months. What on earth happened to cheer you up like this? I checked to see where you were awhile ago, and you were asleep in the swing. Since Johnny and Ruthie were napping, I thought the rest would do you good, so I started to do a little washing. I just finished, and the children are still at their nap. I could use a hot cup of coffee. How about you, Annie? Could you stand a cup of coffee? It might be nice while the house is still quiet."

"Yes, Mama, I would enjoy a cup about now. The weather sure looks ominous out there. The clouds are so heavy and dark. They are really moving fast. I hope Howard reaches home before the wind gets any worse."

"Howard! Was he here? Where did you see him?"

"While I was sleeping, I heard someone call my name. I thought I was dreaming, Mama. But when he touched me and called my name, I realized it was him. I . . . I really thought it was a dream. Mama, he is the same! And he has never married. His father was ill so Howard stayed on the farm to help him out."

"Will he be coming again, Annie. Or was this just in passing by?"

"He was just going by when he recognized me in the swing. He stopped to tell me how badly he felt that I had been through so much. I am so glad he stopped. And yes, Mama, he said he will stop again if he sees me outside."

Chapter 11

Weeks went by before Howard had to go to town for more supplies. As he approached Annie's house he saw her in the yard with Ruthie and Johnny by her side. He stopped to say a few words to her. Not wanting to interrupt her time with the little ones, he meant only to stay a few minutes. As Howard came nearer an apple grazed the side of his arm.

"Hey, there. Apples are to be eaten, not to play ball with. But since you tossed that one, let's see if I can catch the next one. Come on now, throw me an apple, and we will see if I'm as good of a ball player as you are."

Obediently, Ruthie picked up an apple and threw it. Not even coming close to catching it, Howard said, "It's a good thing I stopped by. You will have to teach me how to play catch."

After tossing a few more apples, Howard finally caught one, to Ruthie's delight. "Well, now that I've learned how to play ball with apples, I had better get going."

The Love of Annie

"Don't go, don't go. I want to play ball some more."

Very softly, Howard said, "I want to play ball with you also, but I have some buying to do in town. I have to buy some supplies for my farm and a little feed for my animals. We wouldn't want them to go hungry now, would we?"

"No, I don't want them to be hungry, but I want to play ball with you some more. Please stay and play some more ball with me."

Ruthie didn't want to accept Howard's leaving. She began to cry. Howard, seeing her disappointment over him leaving, reached down and picked her up ever so gently.

"I promise I will come back. I will come again sometime very soon."

"OK then. I will have a whole bunch of apples when you come the next time," Ruthie hollered to Howard as he prepared to leave.

"All right, and when I do get here, we can really play ball."

As Annie said goodbye the little ones both seemed to need attention at the same time. Ruthie wanted to know why that man had to go, and little Johnny needed to be fed. Annie took care of their needs, tucked them in for their naps, then she sat down with a hot cup of coffee. She was happy knowing Howard was back in her life, at least a little bit. Enough to brighten up her day.

After a few days had gone by, Howard decided to ask Annie to be his partner at a square dance. Since she had not danced for so long, she hesitated. Suddenly her mind spun in reverse at the thought of being near Howard again. To be close to Howard while dancing and hearing his voice. She found herself accepting his invitation almost too quickly.

"Annie, I was afraid to ask you to go with me. I was so sure you would say no or find an excuse for not going."

"I'm so happy you asked me to go. A square dance. It's hard to believe I'm going to a square dance."

"Believe it, Annie, just believe it, and hopefully there will be other times to follow."

"It sure sounds good to me," Annie replied.

"We are here already. Looks like they have a good turn out," Howard said as he hurried to get to Annie's side before she climbed out of the buggy. He wanted to be sure he was there to help her.

As they walked into the building neither Annie nor Howard had much to say. Both anticipated the fun they were about to have. Seven years had passed since they had put their romance on hold, and so many changes had taken place in Annie's life. She was excited and happy to be with Howard again, though a bit apprehensive.

As they danced she found herself thinking back to the deep love they had shared before, and how her loneliness was so hard to endure after they parted. Annie also thought of the happiness that slipped away from them when they were sure they would never let it happen to them. She looked up into Howard's face. Her tears were very close to the surface. He kissed her lightly on the forehead and whispered, "Annie, I have never stopped loving you. I promised I would wait for you, and I have waited. I still love you, Annie."

When the dance was over, Howard gently took her hand and walked out into the moonlight. Driving home, they both felt a new joy, a new beginning. Neither wanted to talk. They wanted only to hold onto the magic of this evening. They rode quietly all the way home. Howard kissed her on the cheek, then hurried away, wanting so badly to just hold her in his arms and never let her go.

After that evening, Howard would often show up unexpectedly, and Johnny and Ruthie were overjoyed to see him. They took to him so quickly that his visits became much more frequent than even he himself had anticipated.

Annie once again was feeling like her old self. This puzzled her somewhat because she had been happy with Carper. But this feeling was different, it turned back the pages of time. It was almost as if they had never been apart—such a peaceful feeling!

Every so often, she had to stop and realize that her life had taken a twist for the better at last. Seeing Howard again was all she had thought of for so many years, and now he was here. *He is back in my life again,* she thought. She sang and hummed as she did her work. Even Johnny and Ruthie were more content.

Once Howard saw Annie hanging her wash on the line, and he stopped to say a few words to her. Deep in thought, she jumped from the sound of his voice when he called her name.

"I didn't mean to startle you. I thought you heard me drive up. I'm sorry. What are you so deep in thought about?" Howard asked.

"Well, I . . . I was thinking about our old meeting place. I often long to hear the wind whistle through those pines by our . . . I mean, by the old oak tree," Annie answered.

"Annie, I would love to go there. Will you go there with me?"

"Oh, yes, Howard. Yes, yes. How many times I have longed to see the trees there again and hear the whistling of the wind blowing through them."

"Annie, I never thought it would ever happen. Please, Annie, don't disappoint me. This will be our special night, but I must go now if I want to get my work done."

"Fine, Howard. Goodbye until tonight," Annie said.

"Goodbye," Howard said as he hurried to get on his way.

Evening came much too slowly for Annie. As Howard drove up, she ran to meet him. Both were ecstatic that tonight . . . tonight, they would again be together in their favorite meeting place.

When they arrived at the place where they had met in years gone by, Howard helped Annie from the buggy. For a long moment they stood and looked at the scenery that once they had claimed for their own. The brush had grown, and mounds made from moles or gophers were all around. But the oak trees and whistling pines were still there. As they stood looking at the scenery, they were overcome with emotion. Old memories suddenly came alive.

Howard wrapped his big arms around Annie's tiny waist, and suddenly they embraced. He cupped her face in his tender, but large hands, and couldn't believe he was once again with his Annie. He kissed her tenderly at first. Then, as the fear of losing her again set in, his kisses became as quick and wild as the northwest wind rushing through the pines. Finally, he could not restrain the feelings that were running rampant.

"You must marry me, Annie. Oh, how long I have waited. How I have longed to see you, to hold you. Please, will you marry me?" Howard asked.

"I thought you would never ask. Yes. Yes, of course, I will," Annie said softly.

"Let's set the date soon," he said. "We don't need a fancy wedding, do we? Just being together is all we need. I've

~≪ The Love of Annie

waited so long, Annie! How long I've dreamed of this moment. I hoped and prayed to see you again."

"All right, Howard. I'll tell Mama tonight, then I will tell Johnny and Ruthie first thing in the morning. They love you, Howard, so I'm sure they will be happy. The children do need a good man around the house. It will be nice to have you to help raise them when we are married."

"I love those two, and, Annie, I will try to be the best daddy that I know how to be."

"I know you will, Howard. I'll never have to worry about that."

"Annie, is this really true?" As they looked at each other tears welled up inside of them; they were so overcome with happiness.

"Let's plan a small wedding, but soon," Howard said breathlessly.

"Yes, I agree. We will have a small wedding, and when I tell the good news to Mama, we will start making our plans to get married. Now I'm sure she will be happy for us, Howard, and I know Daddy will be. He has always wanted me to be happy. This will definitely please him.

"I will need a couple of weeks to get things in order. About two weeks, is that OK?" Annie asked.

"Yes, two weeks," Howard replied.

The night was so beautiful, and their love for each other so deep, they didn't talk much, trying to savor this precious time. When they reached home, both were tired, and they decided it was late. Plans for their wedding had to be made, so Howard kissed Annie goodbye and went home. He had so much to do before the day of their wedding. He needed to get to bed a little earlier than usual.

The next morning, Annie could hardly wait to tell her mother the wonderful news. She knew this would please her mother because her mother knew Annie had loved Howard for such a long time.

"Annie, it is good to see you so happy again. This early in the morning and you are up already. Something must be on your mind."

"Yes, Mama. I have something to discuss with you. Do you have a little time?"

"Of course, Annie. What is it you want to talk about?"

"Howard asked me to marry him last night, Mama. I was so happy. I told him yes, I would marry him."

"Did you set the date already?"

"No, we wanted to talk it over with you first and also tell the children. I know they will be happy. They love Howard so much."

"Yes, Annie. Having a father again will be good for the children. And Howard will be a wonderful daddy for them."

"Now that we have a wedding to plan, let's have a cup of coffee and some breakfast. We will make some plans before the children get out of bed."

"Oh, yes, Mama. I would like that."

"I'll talk with Pastor Gates and see what he has on his schedule. Do you have a particular time you would like for your wedding day?" Annie's mother asked.

"I told Howard I would need about two weeks to get ready."

"That sounds about right. I'm sure you will want a small wedding, Annie."

"Yes, Mama, but we will have to have his brothers and sisters. He has a large family, and they live here on the

Martins Ferry Pike. I'm sure they would like to attend the wedding. Howard said whatever date we set will be fine with him, but just make it soon."

When Annie and her mother talked with Pastor Gates about setting a date for the wedding, he was very pleased. "It's about time, young lady, that you married this fine gentleman. I didn't want you to let him slip away again. He is a nice man, Annie! He has a way with so many of the children. They all like him, and he seems to know just what to say to each little one to get a smile from them.

"Well, now, let me see. You want the date to be in two weeks. Fine, fine. That is good timing. I don't have much scheduled, so we will set the date for two weeks from today. June 16, 1916, at 2 P.M. How does that sound?"

"That date is fine. I'm anxious to tell Ruthie and Johnny the good news. I planned to tell them when I told you, Mama, but this is better. With the date being set, they will definitely know we will be married and that they will have a new daddy."

"Oh, Mama," they hollered, when Annie told them they were going to have a new daddy. "When? Mama, when are we going to have a new daddy?"

"Soon, very soon. In only two weeks. Then you can play with him every day."

Howard was anxious to see what date Annie had decided for their wedding day. When she told him the date, he could hardly constrain himself. He thought it was unbelievable that they were going to be together after so much time had passed.

Only the family members and a handful of friends were invited, so on the day of the wedding the little Methodist church had plenty of room for the guests.

After the ceremony was over, they went back to Annie's home for lunch, and to spend a little time with the guests.

Howard and Annie stayed only long enough to be polite, and then they went to his father's home. They planned living with his father for awhile because he was not too well and to help him with his work until they had time to find a home of their own.

When they reached the door, Howard swept Annie up in his arms as they crossed the threshold. This made Annie holler with sheer delight. It brought a smile to her new father-in-law's face. He was happy to see Howard's dreams come true.

A few months later, Annie woke up one morning feeling sick. At first she thought she had the flu, but soon realized she was expecting a child. Howard was happy to think that at long last he and Annie would be proud parents. He was like a schoolboy with a new toy when the baby arrived. They named the little one Elsie. Howard was elated to think they had three children now, and he was a part of it all. Happiness filled their home. Being together, talking over past events, and looking forward to the future fulfilled their lives.

Chapter 12

When Howard came in for dinner, he announced happily that he had found a home. "It is a farm house on top of a big hill. Annie, it is our dream home. You'll love the woods and the fields, and you will love the house! Our home, our very own home! The hill, this great big hill! The house sits right on top of the hill. Annie, it is so nice. It has a big yard for the children to play in, and each can have their own room."

"Oh, Howard, I'm so excited. I'm so happy. How soon can we move?"

"Uh, . . . probably next week. Yes, I think we will be ready to move by the middle of next week. I'm sure we can have everything ready by then."

True to Howard's expectations, they moved into their new home just a few days sooner than he had predicted. The children enjoyed the extra large yard to run and play in. Having a new daddy to climb on and play with, fulfilled their days.

~≈ The Love of Annie

Both Annie and Howard worked hard, gardening, planting flowers, and of course, farming the land. Every day seemed like a new beginning. There were so many jobs to be done. Their days were so full and happy, the time went almost too fast. They were forever thinking of what the other one would want, and they tried to do all the things they had missed out on in the past. Caring so much, they wanted to make up for lost time.

"Tomorrow is Sunday," Howard said. "Sunday is my day, Annie. Every man needs one day to call his own. Is that agreeable with you?"

"Yes, but just what are your plans?" Annie asked, with a puzzled look on her face.

"Well, I have to show you what a good cook I am."

"You mean, you are going to do the cooking?"

"Yes, I have to put some meat on those bones of yours. You have lost weight these past years, so I plan to fatten you up a bit. You need a rest, and Sundays will be a catch-up day for you."

"Oh, I love being spoiled," Annie replied.

"We will have breakfast, attend our church service in Harrisville, and when we get home, I'll show you what a good cook I am. I like to cook, Annie. I did a lot of cooking before we were married. My mother was ill so much of the time the last years before she died, so I helped her with the cooking and housework, and my father did most of the farm work."

True to his word, Howard did the cooking on Sundays, and when dinner was over, they would take the children for a walk. There was a path leading by snarled, but beautiful, trees in the woods. How they looked forward to Sundays.

The Love of Annie

Times were not good. There was not much money to be had. When the children were napping, Howard would say, "Annie, do you think we can slip out for awhile and go rabbit hunting? We will go just a short ways into the woods, so we can keep an eye on the children."

They both loved the woods and the sport of hunting. Besides, it gave them extra food, something a little different to eat. Howard taught Annie how to shoot a rifle. You could hear their laughter ringing through the trees when she missed her target. Annie could hit everything but the target. Once she learned how to shoot the gun, she could hit most anything she aimed at. When kidding about their hunting escapades, her nickname was "Dead Eye." Howard loved to watch Annie when she aimed at something. She would get intense, but seldom did she miss. Annie learned very quickly how to use the gun, to Howard's delight.

The days went by so fast, being happy was all they wanted. To be with each other, to be loved, and to have their own home fulfilled them.

Johnny and Ruthie loved their little sister Elsie. Ruthie would beg to carry her when they were out for a walk. "Mama, can I carry Elsie?"

"I think she is too heavy for you to carry, Ruthie."

"No, Mama, I can do it. I'll be careful. I won't let her fall."

"Ruthie, you can carry her a short way, but then you will have to let her walk."

"OK, Mama. I will put her down when I get tired."

"Howard, we will just have to stop and check on her every so often. She loves her little sister so much. I'm sure carrying her a short ways won't hurt her. Ruthie will be a big help to me when she gets a little older.

"Why are you stopping so often, Howard?"

"Oh, I don't know. I'm wondering if Ruthie is not a wee bit too young to be carrying a child. You know her back is not developed that strongly yet. I guess I want to be sure she doesn't suffer later when she is older. Ruthie is only seven years old. That is too young to lift something that heavy."

"She will be fine. We won't let her carry her too far. Only a few feet. It will make her feel she is helping us."

"Such happy days, our time goes by so swiftly. It is hard to believe how fast the days fly. There never seems to be enough hours in a day for us. Mom, I am so lucky to have such a nice family." (Howard began calling his beloved Annie, *Mom*, after the three children were a mite older.)

"You know, Mom, every day I went back to our meeting place, hoping you would be there. The walk back seemed so much farther. Alone and frustrated that we had let our life slip away like that, I felt so low and depressed. How many times I could hardly pass by without dashing in to convince you we belonged together. I didn't want to push you into marrying me and then find it would frighten you all over again. How that scoundrel Bronson could have treated you so cruelly, I'll never know."

"We are making up for lost time now, Howard. You are the best one to help me. I can't believe I have almost forgotten how badly Bronson treated me. We have our whole life to make up for those years, so let's not waste any more of our time talking of Bronson," Annie replied.

"Yes, Mom, and I would say it is about time, and I could not be any happier then I am right now. For so long I thought

I would never see you again. My prayers are answered," Howard exclaimed.

"Yes, prayer gets us through each day. Now with our new baby, Viola, another little mouth to feed, I worry if we will have enough food to feed us all."

"Annie, if the mines would have work for us, even if only a couple days a week, we could get by."

"Howard, how soon will we butcher a hog? Don't we butcher in August or September?" Annie asked.

"Yes, Mom, they are ready by September. At least we will have meat, and our garden is looking good. With vegetables, pork, and plenty of milk to drink, we will have plenty to eat. The worry is not quite as devastating as other times. With a few days work in the coal mine, it will keep what we need on the table for now."

"Howard, so often I start fretting about the Great Depression people are forever talking about. Everyone you talk with has this on his mind. Right now we are OK, but the meat will last such a short time. The coal mines are giving the workers less and less hours lately. They are lucky to get a couple days work a week," Annie said.

"I know, Mom. I think of it all the time, but we have to try not to worry too much. It can't get much worse then it is."

Howard had to leave for work at the coal mine before daylight, so Annie would sometimes slip back into bed for a little extra rest, until the children got up. She awoke one morning to a knock at the door. Because they lived on farmland, strangers rarely stopped by. As she opened the door, a man stood there. "May I step inside for a moment?" he asked.

"Of course. Please excuse my manners. Please do come in."

"Well ma'am, I'm afraid I have some bad news." Annie's heart began to pound from fear of what she was about to hear.

"What kind of bad news?" Annie asked quickly.

"Well, I'm afraid your husband has been hurt in the coal mines. A couple hours ago there was a cave in, and he was injured."

Annie turned very pale. Her thoughts raced back to when Carper died of injuries from being crushed in the mines. Suddenly, she felt faint. Her thoughts began to race ahead, her mind running wild, fearing the worst again had happened.

"Please! Please, listen to me! He is injured and needs care, but it is not life threatening. Please, please try to keep calm. I'm sure he will be OK, but he is in dire pain right now. The doctor is with him, and he is doing all that he can to help him," the visitor said.

Finally she got control of herself. "How bad is he hurt?" she asked.

"He will be OK," he said as he gently put his arm around her shoulder. "He will be OK." The doctor fears his back is broken, but he said he is quite sure no other injuries occurred. He is in a lot of pain, and he has to stay in the hospital awhile. The doctor feels he can come home in a few days, but he will have to lie very still. With you watching over him, the doctor thinks he will improve in only a few weeks. At any rate, he will be all right," the man exclaimed as he gently put his arm around her shoulder again to comfort her fears.

The Love of Annie

"It will depend on if he has other injuries or not, and of course how badly his back is injured. That's all the doctor could tell us at this point. He does not know yet how long Howard will be laid up. At this time, he can't be certain. Now try not to worry. He should come along fine."

Relieved to know he would be well after a few weeks, she thanked him and made ready for Howard's return. Howard was hospitalized for three weeks before he was released to go home.

"Annie, he will have to be kept quiet and lie still for a couple weeks. Howard can't do anything until his back is healed," the doctor told her, before she took Howard home from the hospital.

When Howard was brought in and put to bed in the living room beside a big potbellied stove, Annie was overjoyed to be able to watch over him. It was so good to have him home again. Annie kept the stove hot with red coals to be sure to keep Howard from getting a chill. She was so happy to have him back home and alive. She remembered only too well when Carper was hurt. She thought he was on the mend when peritonitis set in and he died. Now she thought, *Howard, too, but this time Howard will live! He has to live!* She hurried to get a little food into his body. "You need some good nourishment. With a full stomach you will feel better."

Chapter 13

Days went by, and Howard was in great pain from his injury. He couldn't move. He had to lie in one position until the healing had a good start and the pain subsided. The house was so cold; they kept the stove full of coal to keep warm. One day the temperature dropped to an all-time low. Annie fired the old stove more often than usual. She knew Howard had to be kept warm, because he had to lie so still and not move around. She was afraid his circulation would be poor, so she fired the stove more often then usual to make sure he was comfortable.

As Howard lay in bed thinking how good it would be to get well and to work again so he could bring home a few pennies to help with the added expenses, little two-and-a-half year old Elsie got too close to the hot stove. Her dress caught fire. Howard tried and tried to no avail to reach her. With excruciating pain in his back, he could only lie there helpless as he saw the flames engulf his little girl. He cried

~ The Love of Annie

aloud, "Johnny! Johnny! Get her. Don't let her go outside. Get her, Johnny. Oh, oh grab her!"

Johnny, only a small child himself, ran after Elsie, and as a small child would do, he pulled her to the floor. Annie ran from the kitchen to see Elsie's hair and face burned, her little arms hanging beside her. She worked feverishly to beat out the flames that had burned the clothes off of Elsie's little body.

Fear welled up inside Annie as she tried to get the fire from burning Elsie even more. She was determined to save her little girl. She beat the flames out with her bare hands. She was so frightened she might not be able to save her, she did not realize her own hands were also being severely burned. Elsie screamed from the horrible pain of the burns, and Annie tried with every ounce of love and protection she could muster to settle her down. She did everything she could until Dr. McCleaster, the old family doctor, could get there.

The doctor had just left a few minutes earlier from checking on Howard's condition. He was at the bottom of the hill when he heard the bloodcurdling screams. He hurriedly turned around and went back to see what happened. He couldn't believe what he saw when he arrived. He worked fast to ease the excruciating pain for the little girl.

After taking care of her burns, he looked up at Annie. "Well, well! You are quite a lady. Let me take a look at you. Annie, your hands are bad, really bad. The flesh is just hanging. Let me tend to them or you will surely have more trouble then you can handle. One thing you don't need is infection. You will have your hands full with Elsie's burns. I did the best I could do for your little girl. She will definitely carry scars—more scars then I like to think about, but she will be all right. She is severely burned, and we will have to watch her very closely. As for you, let's take a closer took. Well, I can see you will need a lot of help around here. I'm glad Ruthie can be of some help.

"Annie, I'm so glad I came today to check on Howard's condition. I could hear the commotion way down the road. I was almost to the Webster schoolhouse when I heard this terrible screaming coming from Elsie. I knew something terrifying had happened, so I turned and came back as fast as I could. Lucky I did. I still have some more house calls to make, and you would not have been able to reach me."

"We are surely thankful you were that close by when it happened," Annie told the doctor as he bandaged her burned hands.

"There Howard is, immobilized from his back being injured. Elsie has been burned so badly, and now my own two hands are burned and have to be wrapped. My, oh my! Viola is too young to be weaned, and she has to be fed. Breast feeding her is sure going to be hard to do," Annie said aloud.

Ruthie heard her Mama's remark. "I can help you, Mama. I can help you feed our baby!"

"Ruthie, if you can help me to get the nipple into Viola's little mouth I can manage." Ruthie did the best she could to help Mama feed the baby.

"There is always so much for you to contend with," Howard said as he lay helpless, unable to help at all with his little girls or Annie's pain. "Here you are, Mom, with both of your hands so badly burned," Howard said sadly. "Mom, I can't believe you can love me, yet with so many heartaches. It isn't fair to you."

Annie went to his bedside, leaned over, and kissed him tenderly. Howard, not wanting Annie to know how sad he was, reached out to hold her. Tears burned his eyes and ran down his face. Such love he had for his Annie. Annie tried to pat him on the forehead, but with her hands bandaged from the burns, she could not do it. She wanted so badly to show how much she cared for him, so she leaned closer and whispered, "I'm all right. Quit fretting about me, I am fine."

"All that I have given you are our children and all the heartaches that go along with raising a family. I was so sure of happiness. I was so sure we would make it. I wanted so badly to give you a good life, Mom." He could not hide his heartbreak any longer. He began to cry as he had never done before.

"Howard, Howard. Being with you and the children is all that I need. As long as we have each other and the children are OK, that's what matters. So forget about me. Now let's get some rest. Who knows what tomorrow will bring."

"Well, we are long past due for something good to happen," Howard said.

"We'll take one day at a time," Annie replied as she leaned over to comfort him. "With so much happening this rapidly, we don't have time to worry about hardships do we? I shudder to think what would have happened to Elsie if Dr. McCleaster had not driven out to check on you and heard the bloodcurdling cries from our little girl. He turned his buggy around quickly and headed back to our house. He was so dismayed at the sight of her.

"Then he noticed my hands and insisted I needed help, also. He did so much for you when you got hurt, and he is so thorough in his checkups. He knows we can't pay him for awhile, but he never gives us a bill. Howard, he knows you are going to pay him as soon as you can get hold of a little extra money. I can't help but feel we were still lucky.

She could have been burned much worse. I'm surely grateful. Johnny was so quick to grab Elsie before she got outside. The wind would have caused the flames to be even worse," Annie said.

"My, oh my! I wonder what else can happen to us. Guess we have to take the bitter with the sweet," Howard said as he closed his eyes, trying to block what had just happened out of his mind.

Chapter 14

The older children played with their little sister constantly to help to get her mind off of the pain.

With each day that passed, Annie and her little girl improved. The doctor knew Elsie would have scars, so he was anxious to see the depth of them. When he changed the bandages, Annie was relieved to know there was no infection. Her burns were deep but were healing.

"Annie," the doctor said, "Elsie is going to have some nasty scars that will stay with her perhaps the rest of her life. The really bad scars are close to her hair line and under her little arms. The others will not be so prominent-looking once she is a bit older. Scars can be depressing to anyone and especially a young girl. When I come by next week, we'll see if we can take the bandages off. By then the burns will have healed enough, and it is good to let air get to the burns. Now, young lady, I want to take a look at you. How did you manage feeding Viola with so many bandages?"

"Well, Doctor, it wasn't so bad. Ruthie helped me put my nipple in Viola's mouth. I put a pillow on my lap so she would be up a little higher to nurse. It worked out quite well. When she was through nursing, Ruthie would put her in bed. Without her help, I couldn't have fed Viola. She was so much help. Johnny also helped. He ran so many errands for me, and he stayed by Howard's side so much of the time. With help from the children, we managed quite well. Johnny brought water to his daddy, and his doing odd jobs saved a lot of steps for me."

"Both of you are doing fine. I will check back once more in a couple weeks to make sure the burns are no longer a threat to either of you," the doctor told Annie as he was leaving.

"And, Howard, with all the commotion, I must say you are doing exceptionally well. I would say you could start walking a few steps at a time now. Rest often, and don't you even think of lifting anything yet. No heavy lifting, do you understand? Don't you do anything strenuous for at least six more weeks."

"I'm so happy to be back on my feet again, Doctor, you can bet I will take care of myself. I have to get back to work as soon as I can if we want to eat around here."

As the doctor waved goodbye, Howard and Annie couldn't believe he did not ask to be paid at least a little for the many times he had been there to check on them. The doctor knew they could not possibly have any money. On occasion, Howard would say, "I will pay you for all of these calls one day, but Doctor, I have no idea when I'll be able to do it."

"Never mind, Howard. I was close by. I'll drop in to check on you whenever I pass close enough by your house. There is no charge for this call today."

The Love of Annie

Though it gave Howard some relief to know the doctor was so kind, it weighed heavily on his mind. He was an honest man, and he expected to pay everyone he owed money, no matter how long it would take him to do it.

Two weeks went by fast. The doctor stopped again to see how Howard was doing and to check on Annie and the little one's burns. As he took off the bandages he remarked, "I have a full time job right here. If you didn't have bad luck, you would have no luck at all. I know you surely have had your share. Maybe life will start going better for you now. I'd say it is time!" Dr. McCleaster added.

"I'll say amen to that, doctor. I hope you won't have to come back for a long time," Howard told the doctor as he was about to leave.

Bobby was born two years after Viola. Annie was thinking how tiny a newborn baby is and immediately remarked how they will have to watch the other children, so they don't pick him up and drop the little fellow. "The kids love him already," Annie told Howard.

"Yes, I know, and Annie, I'm glad we had a little boy this time. He can carry on the DeVault name."

"I sort of figured it would please you to have a boy. I think most couples like a boy first, though I can't see why."

Though Howard loved Johnny and Ruthie (as she was called) every bit as much as any father could love his very own, he was happy to share a son with Annie. He never once thought of Johnny and Ruthie as not being his own. To him, they were his children without any reservations. If any one as much as hinted any differently, he was quick to tell them they are his children. "It is how much you love and care for them is what makes a father," he'd say. "A name is only a name, and no one could love them more than I do."

"Howard, you have such a way with the children. You make each one feel he or she is your favorite child. They each think they are so special, each one loved far more then the others. It's amazing how you do this," Annie told Howard, when they were discussing the children.

Annie's love for her family kept her going. "With a family like ours, we are bound to have problems, but we will make it."

"Yes, Mom, somehow we will make it."

"Oh my! What is Elsie screaming about?" they said, almost simultaneously.

"Viola is getting eaten up! Viola is getting eaten up! Mama, hurry! Hurry, Mama. She is crying hard."

Both Howard and Annie ran to Viola's side. Bees—yellow jackets—covered her body. Working fast, Howard yelled, "Mom, run! Run! Drop to the ground! Drop to the ground. I'll get them off of her! Run. I'll get them! I'll get them!"

After he also was stung over and over again, Howard freed Viola from the bees. Her little body was stung so badly you could not touch a spot on her body that didn't have a sting.

Viola became very ill. The doctor did all he could as she lay fighting off the poison in her system. It took a few days before the medicine began to take effect. "This new medicine will help keep infection from setting in. And this salve will make her more comfortable. It will erase most of the pain," the good doctor explained.

Finally, the swelling began to go down, and she got better. "We certainly don't have any dull moments in this house," Annie said one day, when she and Howard were discussing their life on the farm.

"Mom," Howard said, "as if we don't have enough problems, now we are expecting another baby soon. Our timing is the same. There are approximately two years between each of our children. I used to dream of having a house full of kids, hearing their laughter, and of the joy of watching them grow. So often when we were separated, I would lay awake at night, thinking how I wished you were beside me."

"I did the same thing, Howard. So often I thought I couldn't face another day without you."

"Well, Mom, those sad days are behind us now. At long last we have our family, which we both dreamed about."

"Yes," Annie said, "those days are gone, but I am not feeling so good right now. Maybe you had better get Dr. McCleaster. I think our baby will be here soon."

"I will hitch up the horse and buggy and be on my way, Annie. I'll be back with the doctor soon. Try to stay quiet until I get back."

When Howard returned, he hurried to Annie's room. "Mom, are you all right? I hurried, but, Mom, Dr. McCleaster is out on a call, so I left a message that our baby is about to arrive. Mrs. McCleaster said he should be home soon, and she will send him on his way as quickly as she can. I'm so glad I got back in time. I sure dreaded to leave you here alone with the children. When I told them to check on you, but not to bother you, you should have seen their faces. They were so happy to know they would be getting a new baby soon. I made it clear they should just check on you and not ask any questions."

"You must have made your point clear to them. Every five minutes one of them tiptoed to the door and peeked in. Then I could hear them whispering to each other, but they never said a word."

"Well, well. How is my favorite patient doing today? Are your pains close and severe?" the doctor interrupted as he entered her room.

"Yes, doctor. I think the baby will be here even sooner than I thought."

"I have hot water ready and towels and blankets. Is there anything else I should get for you for the delivery?" Howard asked, anxious for this ordeal to end.

"No, no. I'll holler if there is anything I need," the doctor said. "Just stay close in case I should need a little assistance."

"I'll be right here if you need me."

"Well, I guess you are right. You had better stay right here. This one is not wasting any time in making its entrance. Yes, yes. The baby will be here in only a few minutes."

Ethel was born a short time after the doctor got to Annie's bedside.

"Oh she is pretty!" Howard exclaimed. "Mom, she has your beautiful brown eyes, and look at that hair. It already has a tendency to be curly. With a little care, it will be curly. She is another Annie! She will be the apple of everyone's eye, just like you were, or I should say, just like you are."

"You surely have a way of knowing how to build up my ego," Annie quipped, looking down at her little newborn baby.

"No one could ever pass by without noticing how pretty you were, so this one is going to be another Annie," replied Howard.

How Annie loved to sit and curl Ethel's hair around her fingers, when she got a little older. Ethel captured everyone's heart. Cousins brought her candy from the time she was old enough to eat it. They didn't seem to realize the other children would feel neglected not getting candy also. If

Annie or Howard were near when the candy was given out, they would make her share it. Ethel didn't like all the attention, so on occasion she would hide under the bed. But she made sure she had her candy before she would disappear.

"Where did Ethel go?" the cousins asked.

"Oh, she is around here some place," Annie would tell them, hoping they would not pursue looking for her any more. Annie realized Ethel was not happy with so much attention, so she tried to discourage some of it.

When Gladys entered the world on a chilly November day, the children all wanted to be the first one to hold her. Ethel was still very young and was right there by Mama's side most of the time, wanting to be a part of her little sister's life. She was only a little more than two years older then the newest arrival and was a little demanding in wanting to help to take care of her.

"I want to do this, can I? I want to help you."

"OK, OK. You can get the diaper. Go now and get it before she gets cold. We don't want our baby to get sick."

The older ones let Ethel help whenever they could, although it became very annoying to them because it took so much longer for their work to get done.

A lot of people had large families. But Howard and Annie's family was one of the larger ones, and it added to their problems with jobs so hard to find.

The children kept Annie's mind occupied. Gladys was the youngest, the seventh child, and she added to their hardship. She kept Annie's mind and body exhausted. Annie wasn't one to complain and always used her quick wit to keep from giving up. But too much had happened in her young life, and the stress had taken its toll.

Annie suffered a heart attack and needed rest but had no place to go, so her sister Elda came to help her through the ordeal.

"Annie, you need help. I am going to take you to our house so you can get the rest you need. You have to get away from the children until you get better. I will pack your things quickly, then get you settled in."

"Yes, I know I need rest. Hopefully I can get stronger soon and not be a burden to you."

"Nonsense, that's what a sister is for, isn't it? We have the extra bedroom next to my room. I can hear you if you need me. I'll have your things ready in a minute, then I'll take you home with me until you are well again," Elda said.

Gladys wasn't yet weaned from nursing and refused to eat after Annie had gone to her sister's house to get rest. Ruthie and Elsie tried over and over again to get some food into the little one, but she would not let them get a bite of anything in her mouth. They were so afraid she would get sick if they didn't get a little nourishment in her tiny body.

At long last, they got her to swallow a wee bit of food. It was such a relief for them. "Elsie, our baby ate a little food! Maybe we can get her to eat some more in a little while," Ruthie hollered, with excitement.

"Do you think our baby will be OK?" Elsie asked.

"I think she will be all right now. We got her to eat a little."

"I'm scared. I don't want her to die, Ruthie."

"She won't die, Elsie. Now she will be OK. Little babies don't need as much as we do, but they have to eat something. Mama was nursing her, so our baby didn't know how to eat this way. That's why I got so scared when she wouldn't eat anything."

The Love of Annie

When Howard saw Annie, he was anxious to tell her how well the girls took over the responsibility with the baby. "Mom, it was quite a responsibility taking care of the little one with no mother to nurse her. This seemed so impossible for the two girls, Ruthie, barely fourteen years old, and Elsie only nine. They are just children themselves. But Mom, they tried so hard to tend to Gladys the best way they knew how, to give her the care that was needed since you got sick. There was just no other way. You would be proud if you saw how they handled our baby."

"I knew Ruthie would handle her well. She is so capable for her age," Annie replied, "and Elsie is a good little helper."

Annie began to show signs that she was improving from her heart attack. She got stronger each day and was anxious to get back home to be with her family.

At the age of thirty-five, Annie often felt she had already lived a lifetime. Her strong determination kept her going. Also, her beautiful sense of humor and love for everyone helped to ease some of the stress.

After weeks had passed, Howard brought his beloved Annie home, only to find that life still had more tough blows to hand them. As Annie was resting, trying to gain back her strength, Elda's deaf husband burst into the house, leaned over Annie's shoulder, and said ever so loudly, "Guy is dead! Guy is dead! Did you hear me, Annie? Guy is dead! He got killed in Hell's Kitchen Coal Mines!" Because he was deaf, he yelled so loud. Annie jumped up.

"Sylvan, that's not true. That can't be true. Not Guy! Please say it's not true. Not Guy! Not my dear brother Guy! Not . . . not Guy!"

"Yes, Annie, it's true. He is dead!"

~≈ The Love of Annie

Annie stood motionless, staring into space, trying hard to dispel this awful thought. Carper had died from injuries in the mine. Howard had his back broken in a coal mine also, and now Guy. "It can't be true. It can't be! Not Guy too."

"It's true, Annie. You might as well accept it," Sylvan told her. "You have to accept it because it happened. He is dead! Poor Gwen. She has two children to raise alone now, and her new baby on the way will never know his daddy."

By this time, Annie was also pregnant again. With the heart attack, the new pregnancy, and now her beloved brother Guy getting killed in the coal mines, she was so distraught, it was almost too much for her to bear. Because Ethel was so young, and Gladys not too far behind, Annie tried to bear up. "I must not give into feeling sorry for myself," she thought as she tried to choke back the tears.

Her brother Guy was the one who had been there for her when she needed someone to talk to. He was close by to reassure her or just be there when she needed someone to comfort her and to show his deep love for his favorite sister. She knew Howard was always by her side, but Guy was her brother and friend from a small child on. "I have always relied upon him," she said aloud. "Now he is gone!"

Annie could not hold back the hurt any longer. She began to cry uncontrollably. The pain was so unbearable. She couldn't hide the sadness she felt because her beloved brother had also been killed. "Guy, Guy, I can't believe it. I'll miss you so much," Annie said to herself.

The doctor came to comfort Annie and to be with her in case he was needed. Her heart was so bad; he was concerned this bad news could cause more trouble. The older children tried to keep the younger ones quiet and playing outside as much as possible.

Howard's family came to see Annie when they heard that Guy had been killed. This pleased Annie. She always enjoyed them when they came. Of course, her cousin remembered to bring candy for Ethel, no matter what the reason was for them coming to visit. He brought some this time also, and Ethel took the bag and ran. But Gladys saw where she went and followed her to the bedroom. When Ethel hid under the bed, Gladys lay on her stomach and begged for some of her candy. Ethel, trying to hide from these cousins so they would not pick her up, tossed some of her candy out from under the bed to get rid of Gladys. She kept hoping they would not find her. Gladys lay there until the candy was all gone, and Ethel got mad.

"Get out of here! You ate all of my candy! See it's all gone. I don't have anymore. See here is the bag. It's gone! My candy is all gone."

"Candy all gone?" Gladys asked.

"Yes, it's all gone. Now go away. I think Mama wants you. You'd better go."

"OK," Gladys said, and out she went.

Ethel stayed under the bed until the company had gone home. Just to be alone without people fussing over her is what she wanted.

"Let's go out side and play for awhile," Ethel said to the others, when she came out from under the bed. Bobby was always ready to do something new, so he agreed quite readily.

"Hey, Ethel, let's go down by the pigpen and play. We can give the pigs some corn, then we will climb up on the fence and watch them fight over it."

"OK," Ethel said. "I'll race you down to the fence. One, two, three, let's go!"

Bobby started running, and as they neared the fence, Bobby seated himself nicely on top of the fence with one quick motion. "I beat! I beat you."

"Well, you should beat. You're a boy!" Ethel hollered. About that time, Ethel made it to the top of the fence also but lost her balance and fell headfirst into the pigpen. Bobby laughed and laughed so hard. It made Ethel feel bad, but this didn't stop him. Since she was pretty, it tickled him to see her all full of mud.

"Quit laughing," the older ones yelled. "That's not funny. The pigs could have eaten her! They could have eaten her all up!" Bobby laughed so hard he couldn't talk.

"Shut up, Bobby! We said that the pigs could have eaten her all up."

"Why would the pigs want to eat Ethel? Yuk! I think they would like corn better then her!" When Bobby thought even the pigs would not like her, this made the others laugh.

Ethel didn't know why the others were laughing, so she went to see herself in the mirror. When she saw she was full of mud, she felt better. *That's why they were laughing at me. I'm so dirty,* she thought. Ethel brushed herself off and went back out to play.

Chapter 15

With seven little mouths to feed, Howard and Annie did not have enough money to live on. The food they had from the garden was getting scarce. There was no money to buy clothes or any of the much-needed articles to raise a family, barely enough to keep going. Their worries seemed to never end. Knowing how low they were on food for the family added more stress.

"Mom," Howard said, "I don't know what to do. I don't know where to go. How I wanted to give you nice things." Tears burned his eyes as he tried to talk. "I must see if I can find work. I will go to town and see what I can find. Maybe some one will give me a day's work. The blamed coal mines are always striking. I have to find a job."

When morning came, Howard started out to look for work. Annie felt better while he was gone, so she planted her flowers. She loved flowers and kept her seed from one year to the next. She made sure she could enjoy her flower garden even through hard times. As the day wore on, Annie

~≈ The Love of Annie

kept busy physically and by thinking of Howard. Hoping he would get a day's work somewhere kept her mind busy.

She was deep in thought when Ethel and Bobby ran to the kitchen. "Mama! Mama! Daddy's here. He is coming up over the hill."

"That's good. Maybe Daddy found a job today."

"Found a job! Did Daddy find a job? Could we find one too?"

"Someday, children, but for now you are a mite too young," she told them, smiling to herself as she patted them on their head.

As Howard approached the door, his head hung low, his shoulders slumped. By the worried look on his brow, Annie knew he had not found work. He was full of despair.

"There was no work," he said. "I went everywhere. No one needed anything done. I will go again tomorrow."

"Howard, please try not to worry so much. I know we will be all right. You will find work somewhere. You work so hard; someone will give you a day's work. When we pray, we will ask for God's help. He has never let us down. We have to live one day at a time, Howard. He has a reason for everything."

"Yes, Annie, I know he has a reason for everything, and God does know what is best for us. I guess I love my family so much, I sometimes feel worthless when I can't make enough money to feed them."

"Howard, this is not your fault. It is this Great Depression people are talking about that is making it so hard for everyone."

They sat down to beans and biscuits. After eating all the beans, there was hardly a thing left in the house, except flour to make a few pancakes, which would keep a little food in the tiny stomachs.

"How I wish just once we would not have to worry where our next meal will come from, Mom."

"Yes, Howard. It is a big worry. We have to feed the children somehow, but we will find a way. Yes, we will find a way."

Annie talked as if she were trying to convince herself. Neither of them wanted to make the other any more upset than necessary. Each tried to hide his or her fears and was very thankful for when they could butcher a hog and when their cow would have her calf. Then the children would have milk and meat. The meat didn't last long when they did butcher, with so many mouths to feed.

The meager amount of money Howard earned was never quite enough to pay the extras, not enough for a doctor when one of the children was ill, and there was seldom a penny to pay the payment on the farm. Bills kept mounting and mounting. Annie grew very tired, but she never complained. Her sweet smile and loving ways kept Howard going. Also, the little Methodist church they attended regularly was a blessing to them. The minister often prayed a special prayer for those who needed help. He knew that with a family the size of Howard's there could not be enough money to go around. His extra prayers made Howard and Annie feel that, along with the help from God, there was someone else who also understood the dilemma they were in and wanted so badly to help ease some of the stress they were experiencing. They made every effort possible to instill in their children where their help comes from.

Praying was one thing that was a part of their everyday living. "Now, we want the same for our kids," Howard told

Annie. "When we can't attend church, we must see that our kids get there regularly. They can stop at Mrs. Wilson's home and wash their feet. She said they could wash them under their pump. Walking barefoot that far will save on their shoes."

After supper each night, Howard played with the children and then turned into bed. Each morning he left early to find work. Each day seemed a lifetime, and each night he came home feeling more depressed than he had the day before. "Our kids have to have food, and we have nothing left in the house to feed them. My, oh my. What can I do? I don't know where to turn anymore, Mom."

"Howard, I know. I know. We don't have enough food to feed us all another meal. There isn't enough to go around. Howard, what are we going to do?"

"Let's get some rest. Maybe we can find a way when morning comes," Howard told Annie as he tossed around, trying to put the stress aside.

After a restless night worrying how he could feed his family, he got up early in the morning. "Mom, isn't today the day that Elda planned to have her picnic?"

"Yes, that is right. She is having it today. But Howard, I don't have anything to take along."

Howard spoke very softly, "Mom, we could let Ruthie and Johnny go to Elda's for her picnic and the rest of us could stay home. They could take the short cut through the fields, and if they eat their dinner there, we could perhaps stretch what little food we have among the others."

"Yes," Annie said. "Yes, maybe we have enough to go around for the little ones. Not as much as we need, but at least they won't go to bed hungry. I'll tell Ruthie and Johnny to get ready so they will be there in time for dinner."

The two children didn't want to go. They wanted to stay at home. They were too young to realize there was not enough food in the house to feed them. Both Howard and Annie knew something had to be done. Annie looked sadly at Howard, trying not to show how badly she felt or the worry that was mounting each day in her bosom. They both knew some would go to bed very hungry if they all ate at home. Sending the two older children to their aunt's house was absolutely the only way to get through another day.

To ease little Johnny and Ruthie's minds about why they had to go to their aunt's house when none of the others were going, Annie told them, "Your Aunt Elda wants to see you. I know you would rather stay at home, but we want to make your aunt happy, don't we? You don't have to stay long. We love you too much to have you stay too long. After dinner, just tell your aunt you want to come back. She will understand. Darkness sets in earlier, and I want you home before it gets dark."

Hesitatingly, the two agreed and started their trek through the fields. They waved goodbye for as long as they could see their farmhouse and their mama waving back to them. Her heart was breaking at the thought of having to send them away because there was not enough food in the house for them to eat.

After the children were gone, Annie tried to hide her grief. She quickly wiped away the tears, not wanting Howard to see her heart so broken. Howard helped Annie divide the little food they had among the rest of the family. There wasn't much, so neither Howard nor Annie felt like eating. They gave the food to the children, hoping it was enough to hold them through the day and help them sleep through the night.

~≪ The Love of Annie

Tired, depressed, and worried, they tucked the little ones in bed and then walked out to the flower garden. Annie stopped and looked up into Howard's sad face. "Please, Howard, don't worry. The older ones can go berry picking tomorrow. I walked by the creek and the berries are quite plentiful. I'll take Johnny, Elsie, and Viola; and Ruthie can stay with the others while we pick the berries."

"Mom, Mom, you work so hard. Tomorrow, yes, tomorrow, I will find something. I must find a day's work." Such a hopeless feeling came over them as they slowly started back to the house.

"Why don't we sit on the porch for awhile. It's peaceful and quiet. The breeze feels soft and warm, and I can smell your roses from here. I love your flowers, Annie. They give me a lift when I'm feeling a little down," Howard commented.

Putting his arm around her waist, they sat quietly. Neither wanted to talk or even mention the hopeless situation they were in. They sat as if waiting for their dreams to come true, for something miraculous to happen so they would not have to leave their home on the hill. The flower garden and sitting on the porch together relieved some of the tension. The quiet beauty that surrounded them was serene. They found a few minutes of happiness, smelling their roses in the evening breeze.

They were so worried about the farm payment. Neither wanted to bring up the subject. They did not want to break the spell of their quiet time alone.

When payment after payment became due without money to pay even the smallest amount on the farm, the landlord came to collect.

Annie and Howard wondered how long it would be before he would show up. It seemed much too soon that he was at their door.

"Oh, Howard," Annie gasped "He is here! What can we do? Where can we go?"

"Now, now, Mom. I will try to get a little more time. I'm sure with you expecting our baby, he won't put us out," Howard said hopefully.

"He surely won't evict us. He . . . he can't. He just plain can't," Annie said sadly.

Howard went to the door to let the man in. They knew he not only wanted a payment, but he wanted all the money that they owed him.

"Howard, I came to collect my rent money for the farm. I have bills to pay also. You must pay me today."

Howard's chest felt so heavy. "I . . . I'm sorry. I'm so sorry. I have worked hard to get money for you, but . . . I can't seem to muster up enough to make ends meet. I will pay you. I promise I will pay you. I don't know how, but I will pay you. Please give me a little while longer, just a little longer, could you please? Things have gotten a little out of hand. With Elsie getting burned, and Viola so badly stung in a yellow jacket's nest, we had been so worried about them. One thing after another. I have no place to take Mom and the children, and Mom is expecting another baby."

"Well," he replied, "I'll give you a few more months, but that's all. Either you have the money, or you will have to move."

"All right, thanks so much. I'll try. I will try to get you a little."

"A little!" he retorted! "I want full payment!" he said as he stalked out the door.

~ The Love of Annie

"Mom, we can stay here yet. We won't have to move until after our baby is born."

"Thank goodness, Howard. Oh, thank goodness. I love it here on the hill so much. Just maybe we will be able to rake enough together by then, and he won't put us out."

On Sunday, after getting home from church and when dinner was over, Howard remarked what a wonderful sermon the minister had. "Mom did you hear his prayer? It sounded so much again like it was a special prayer for us."

"Yes, he always seems to know when our load is a little heavier then usual. He is a good preacher, Howard."

"Annie, do you think you would feel up to going rabbit hunting for awhile? If we are lucky enough to shoot one, we can have it for supper."

"I'm always up to going to the woods. Give me a few minutes to change into something comfortable."

They loved hunting together. It seemed to relieve some of the tension built up after something out of the ordinary happened.

When Annie first learned how to shoot a gun, she hit everything except her target. As time went on, Howard was proud of her ability to hit whatever she aimed at. This pleased Howard, so he began to call her "Dead Eye." They teased about who shot the first rabbit. Howard was happy Annie loved the sport so much and had mastered her shooting so well.

The children knew Mama and Daddy were coming home when they heard their laughter ringing out through the trees. They would run to the edge of the woods to meet them to see if their hunting trip was a success.

Chapter 16

On a Saturday morning, the landlord showed up as expected. Both Howard and Annie knew what he was going to say would not be good. Holding back tears, they welcomed him in.

"Well, Howard, do you have the money for me? I have given you all the time that I can. I want my money."

"With times getting worse and worse, I don't have any money, and I can't seem to get any," Howard said. "You have been most kind, but I just can't seem to make ends meet. Does this mean we have to move?"

"I'm afraid so. You have one month or until your baby is born, then I want the farm back. So you had better start looking for another home. I'm sorry, I don't mean to be cruel, but I want my money. I have to have my money, so you see that I get it! I will be back in one month."

With heavy hearts, they bid him goodbye. Howard and Annie stood motionless, so much sadness in their hearts.

The lack of money and immense problems that go along with trying to raise a big family were bad enough, but having to leave their home on top of the hill, to be evicted from the home they loved so much, was all the more devastating. Losing their first home caused such monumental pain that they clung to each other and cried. They had no where to go for help. Desperate and sad, both felt exhausted and numb. Annie hoped the children would not see them in this state of mind—that they'd stay outside a little longer and play until they could get their feelings under control.

"Howard, we feel so badly, but we must not let our kids feel this awful pain we are going through. There will be time for them to find out the real knocks of life when they are older. We must get on with our preparations to move, with as little of our true feelings showing to protect them from this as much as possible."

"Yes, Mom, I know you are right. We do have to pull ourselves together. Any minute they will be bursting through that door. One thing we don't want is for them to see us upset, and for sure, we don't want them to see us crying. We can't subject them to this.

"How I wish there was some way, just some little thing that I could do to ease your pain. Mom, I love you so . . . so much. I'm sorry to have to put you through this painful thing," Howard said.

"I love you, also, and we will go through it together. Howard, you are hurting as much as I am. We will be all right. This is what they mean when they say it's the sign of the times. This is not anyone's fault. We have had so many hard knocks, and this awful depression is the cause of it all. There are a lot of people out there, who are as poor as we are. Look around us. In this small area alone, there are people like us. We have a larger family than a lot of people have, so that means we have more shoes to buy and more mouths to feed. Everyone is in the same boat as we are. We have to try to make the best of a bad situation," Annie told Howard.

"Shall we see what we can muster up to eat?" was Howard's reply. He sensed the discussion had to end for the children's sake.

"The choices are not too plentiful," Annie quipped as she headed for the kitchen.

"At this point, Mom, we will take what we have, huh!"

"Yes, Howard, and we had better be glad to have these slim pickings."

When Billy was six weeks old, the family moved. With heavy hearts, the two of them stood gazing at the woods and fields surrounding their home. They tried to remember every little thing of the home they loved so much. Hurting too badly to speak, each stood as if in a trance. Such pain they felt, knowing this would be the last time they would ever stand together in their garden among the flowers. Howard bent down and picked a rose. He gently put it in Annie's hand.

They embraced for the last time in their beautiful garden, hot tears running down their faces, and their hearts breaking with sadness. Suddenly a loud burst of thunder broke the silence. Streaks of lightening lit up the sky! The lightening was sharp and the thunder roared with such vengeance, they hurried from the garden and got on their way. The horse and wagon, laden down with their meager belongings and their children, headed away from the home they loved so dearly, to a whole new surrounding. They did not know what the future had in store for them.

They arrived at their new home some hours later. With help from the older children, they settled in before darkness set in. Annie kept busy to ease the pain of leaving her home on the hill. There was too much to do and not any time for self-pity. She worked ever so hard to get settled so they could get on with their lives.

One day, as Annie was going about her work, she heard a loud noise. "What was that? What in the world was that?" She ran to check the older children, since the noise seemed to come from the direction in which they were playing. As she passed where little Billy lay she gasped, "Oh! Oh Billy! Oh Billy!" She ran to where he lay and hollered for the children to come help her. Annie grabbed the baby and ran outside so she could quickly get fresh air into his lungs, for he seemed to be not breathing. Annie held the little thing, fearing he would die in her arms. She prayed, "Please, God. Make him breathe. Please make him breathe. Oh God, he is just a baby. Help him to breathe. Please, please, God. Don't take my baby!"

Just then Billy let out a loud cry. "There, there little one. You are OK. Mama's here, Mama's here." Annie's heart pounded hard for fear she would lose her little one. Her hands trembled as she walked slowly back to the house. "Thank you God, oh thank you! Thank you for saving my baby!"

As she sat holding him, it was such a relief to know he was OK. *Such a fragile little thing*, Annie thought. "Thank you, God, for saving my baby!" she repeated. She was so happy that he was alive. She sat and rocked the little one until she had control of herself and felt calm again.

Soon Annie realized the loud noise she had heard could not have come from little Billy. She immediately began checking what had made the noise that had brought her to her baby's bedside. After looking around, Annie discovered a baseball the older children were playing with had cracked a window. Annie was so grateful for the noise she did not even scold them. She knew the broken window had perhaps saved little Billy's life.

It was such a relief to see the color coming back into his little face. Not knowing this was only the beginning of many similar episodes, Annie was ever so grateful that Billy was all right. Too soon, Howard and she would know something was really wrong with Billy. Too often his body would turn a bluish color. Billy was what the doctor called a "blue baby." He would turn blue from crying. One day he quit breathing completely.

"Mama," Johnny yelled. "I'll make him better! I'll make him better!" Johnny grabbed Billy and ran outside. He didn't want his mama to see her little one so limp in his arms. He could not see Billy breathing at all, and Johnny thought his little brother would die. He shook him gently at first. Then he became so frightened that Billy was dead that he shook him again with a little more force, trying to get him to breathe. Finally, Billy made a loud, gasping sound, and Johnny knew he had saved his little brother's life.

He carried him back into the house, back into his mama's arms. The strain slowly left Annie's tired, but happy face as she waited anxiously, her arms outstretched and a prayer on her lips.

Times seemed to get worse every year. The year of 1928 was rough for everyone. Jobs were even harder to find. With no money, people looked for some way to feed their families. It proved almost too much for Howard to handle, providing food for his family while living in all new surroundings in a farm home near the town of Emerson. This was far more then just a challenge. It was one of the worst fears a man would have to face in his life. Having no money, no job, and no contacts to get a job, was very stressful.

Everything was so different now. Ruthie had been in high school, but she quit school to get married.

"Mama, I will quit school, too. I will find a job and help you and Daddy a little bit," Johnny said quickly.

"We don't want you to quit going to school, honey. We will manage somehow," his mama told him. "I hate to see you quit school, Johnny."

"I want to get a job, Mama. Then we won't have to worry so much."

"Are you sure you want to quit?"

"Yes, I don't like going to school anyway. I'll find a job so I can help you out a little."

Ruthie getting married and Johnny quitting school helped their parents survive the everyday ordeals that kept piling up and was a big blessing to them. Johnny tried to help as much as he could, but there was never enough money to live on. Howard decided he again had to find more work somewhere. As they were readying themselves to call it a day and go to bed, Howard suddenly became very quiet. A deep depression came over him. He looked at Annie's tired face and saw the strain of the past events showing on her brow. It made his heart ache even more.

"Mom, I must strike out tomorrow morning to see if I can find a day's work again. Why, oh why, can't we ever have enough to rub one penny against the other? I will get up early tomorrow, Mom, and I will look for work again. I need a day's work. How it hurts to see you go without hav-

The Love of Annie

ing nice things, and even more, not having enough food to feed my family."

"But, Howard, you try so hard! Don't blame yourself. Everyone is having a rough time. Our country is in bad shape. Please, don't be so hard on yourself."

"Well, I know I have to find work somewhere. Let's go to bed, Mom, and try to forget our problems until tomorrow."

"All right, Howard. I'm sure you will find something. You are right, let's put them out of our minds for now and really try to get some rest," Annie answered.

It didn't matter to Howard that he didn't sleep too well. He was determined to find work! He got up much earlier the next day, going from place to place. Again the task seemed utterly impossible. No one needed a hired hand. He finally stopped at a farmhouse. As he approached the house the farmer met him.

"I'm Mr. Herman. I saw you coming down the road. Could I help you?"

"Yes, oh yes, Mr. Herman. I need work. I am in desperate need of a day's work. I have my children to feed, and sir, we have hardly a bite of food in the house to eat. Could you help me out, sir? I need work. I need work so badly. Please, could you find it in your heart to give me a day's work or so?"

Mr. Herman stood in silence as he studied his visitor. Howard's heart began to pound. *My only hope, my last hope,* he thought as he stood there. Fear began to overtake him. He was so sure he would have to go back and face his loving family with no food, nor hope of any. Then suddenly he thought he was dreaming when he heard Mr. Herman's voice.

"Howard," he said, "you seem like an honest man. Guess I could use an extra hand around here. You can start tomorrow. We will see how it goes."

Overcome with the reality of finding work, Howard could not speak. He just stared ahead.

"Howard. Howard, did you hear what I said? You can start tomorrow."

"Uh, . . . uh . . . oh, my. I . . . I can work for you? Please, sir, did I hear you say I can work for you?"

"Yes, I can use some help around here, so you can start tomorrow."

"Thank you, sir, Yes, . . . yes, I will be here! You can count on it! Oh, yes, I will be here bright and early in the morning.

As Howard turned to go home with his good news of finding a little work, Mr. Herman called to his wife. As she stepped outside he asked her, "Don't you have an extra loaf of bread that you've baked? Our new hired man might enjoy eating some of your fresh baked bread. Perhaps . . ." he said, hesitating a brief moment, "do you think by chance we could spare them a couple loaves tonight?"

"Yes, we have plenty loaves this time. I made a double amount today," she said as she hurriedly went to get the bread.

"Good, good," Mr. Herman said. "I'm sure Howard's family will enjoy your fresh baked bread."

When she returned with the two loaves of bread, Howard said, "Thank you! Thanks! My wife will be so happy tonight, with this bread and fresh berries to eat. Thank you. I promise you won't be sorry you hired me. I'll work hard! I am a good worker, and I won't let you down."

"I'm not worried," he replied. "It's getting late. By the time you reach home, it will be nearly dark, so I will see you in the morning."

"Thanks again so much, Mr. Herman. And thank you, for the bread Mrs. Herman. We most certainly will enjoy this."

Howard got home as Annie was picking a wild flower and counting the petals on it. She looked up, expecting to see Howard's sad face, but he leaned down and swept her off her feet. "Mom, I found a job! I get to start tomorrow!" Howard kissed her tenderly. "It isn't much, Mom, but we will have food on the table."

Happiness overcame them as they sat down on a bench so Howard could tell her all about it before the children discovered their daddy was home.

Hand in hand, they walked to the house. "Fresh bread and berries," Annie exclaimed. "Oh, what a treat!"

The children came out of the house, saw their daddy, and happily ran to greet him. "Daddy! Daddy!" they screamed, when they reached the garden. "Where were you, Daddy?" You were gone away so long. Why did you stay away so long? Why did you stay all day, Daddy? We missed you."

"I thought we needed a little nourishment around here, so I had to see if I could find work."

"Did you find work, Daddy?"

"Yes I did. Now run along to the house if you want to eat something good."

"OK, Daddy," they yelled, as they ran ahead of Howard and Annie, seeing who could get there first.

When the family sat at the table to begin their meal, Howard said, "God! I am so grateful for this food that you have supplied for us. Thank you, Jesus. Too often we fail to call upon you when things are rough, but you are there for us regardless. Thanks for your love and understanding.

"Mom, I think I am so lucky to have a good family. Someday things will get better for us. We have to be patient. Things will get better. Life has a way of turning things around. As you said, we have to be patient," Howard reminded Annie.

Howard awoke early the next morning. He kissed Annie goodbye and left for his new job. His steps seemed to have more bounce to them than on the previous days. He worked hard day after day. The pay was not much, but they had food on the table, and they managed to send the children off to school. They were so thankful the schoolhouse was close enough the children could walk to school. Everything once again seemed to be a little better.

The house was not as lovely as their home on the hill, but knowing there was nothing they could do about their situation, they tried to get on with what was ahead of them. There was no time to sit around feeling sorry for themselves.

One-and-a-half years later, Anna Lee was born, and she weighed only three pounds. She was too tiny to hold in her hands, so Annie carried her on a pillow. With each baby, Annie had love abounding, and she was so proud of each child. Her love always shone through no matter what hardships there were to endure. Anna Lee had to be fed often because she was so tiny. She had to be watched constantly, until she weighed a little more.

"Your lungs are much stronger than your little body," Annie said one day, when Anna Lee cried a little more then usual. She picked her up without the pillow. Annie leaned down and kissed her tiny hand, as if to say, no matter how much you cry, I love you.

Howard worked every hour he could, dividing his working time between the Hermans and another family, also farmers in the area. He also worked in the coal mines when there was work to be had. He often became weary when there was no money to pay the rent. Annie was by his side, regardless of what problems came their way. Life seemed so cruel at times, but Annie never wavered. She constantly looked for a brighter tomorrow, and not once did she let the children feel the stress. She had a loving smile and a gentle touch and was never too busy to take time to listen when a little one was hurt or frustrated about something.

Each night she put her hand lovingly on each child's head as they knelt on their knees to say their prayer. "Now I lay me down to sleep, I pray the Lord my soul to keep. If I should die before I wake, I pray thee, Lord, my soul to take." With a kiss goodnight and her sweet loving words, "Goodnight pet," the little ones would go off to bed feeling happy and secure in Mama's love.

Chapter 17

Howard noticed that Annie was more nervous then usual, but with some help from the older children, she managed to get along quite well with her newborn baby.

1929 was bad, really bad. The Great Depression had hit with such force. The stock markets crashed, and banks were in such bad shape. The few people who had money in a bank could not get it. The banks, also, were in trouble during this awful depression. Many people lost their savings completely.

Annie began to feel hopeless. So many mouths to feed and never enough money to pay the bills began to wear on Annie's nervous system. Knowing they would have to move again if they could not come up with the rent money began to show wear on her kind and happy disposition. In the past, she had never been short-tempered or hard to get along with. She had always tried hard to look on the bright side of everything. But now Howard could see it was getting harder each day for Annie to hide her anxieties.

Times were even worse now than before, and they knew there was not a chance they would have the money to pay the rent. Their worst fear was they would have to find another home soon.

Much sooner than Howard and Annie expected, the landlord was at their door and threatened to evict them. Not having a place to go worried Annie. She cried often. Trying to hide her fears from Howard and the children was not easy. Seeing his Annie cry was so hard on Howard. It was the last thing he wanted to see, his Annie so sad, and he not able to comfort her.

This time the landlord was even more stern and persistent than the one who evicted them from their beloved home on the hill. Four week's notice was all they had. "One month," he said. "One more month is all you have to get the money. Now, Howard, you know that I'm not a mean person. I have tried to be good to you, but where money is concerned, I feel there is a limit. You have gone the limit. Now this is it! I expect my money in four weeks. Do you hear me? Do you understand, four weeks?"

"Yes," Howard said. "I most certainly do understand. I have no place to take my family. We have no place to go. I will do all that I can to get the money for you by then."

"You had better do more than that. You get the money for me or else. In four weeks I will be back!"

They tried so fervently with every ounce of strength and ingenuity they could think of to come up with a little money. Just enough so the landlord might give them a few more weeks. This was just wistful thinking. All of their nice thoughts were to no avail. No matter how hard they tried, they could not find a way to get more money. They had such a small amount when the time came to pay their rent.

Hopefully, they thought, *he might have a change of heart and accept the small amount we can pay.*

The landlord came early one morning, and when he saw the amount of money Howard could scrape up for the rent payment, he said sharply, "That measly amount you have is not one half of what I need. I must tell you, you will have to move somewhere else. This is final. You have to find another place to live immediately. I have waited long enough for my rent money. When I come back, you had better be gone."

Howard went from place to place to find a home for his family to live. Everywhere he went they wanted some assurance, just a little something, to assure them of at least getting some of their money. This he could not begin to do, so he kept looking and looking for somewhere to take his family to have a roof over their head.

There was no place for Howard and Annie to take their family, as hard as they tried. They did not have money to pay the rent, and no one was willing to give them a home. Worry was plain to see in Howard's face. Soon the news began to get around of the dilemma he and his family was in.

Elda, Annie's youngest sister, owned a small house a few miles from where Annie and Howard had been living. When they heard that Annie and Howard had been evicted, they came quickly and offered them this small house to live in.

"Annie, you know we have this little house in Harrisville. It is only three rooms, and it needs a lot of repair. I grant you, it is not much of a house, but it's a place to live for now."

Elda, and her husband, Sylvan, had bought another house. Realizing the terrible predicament Howard and Annie were in, they felt sorry for them and decided to let them have this modest little house. It was not nearly large enough for such a big family, but it was a place to live—a roof over their heads that they could call home again.

"Elda, we can't thank you enough for what you have done. How I wish we could show you how grateful we are. We have a home for our family to live in because of your kindness. Thank you, Elda and Sylvan, thank you so much. There are no words to say how much this means to us."

"I'm glad it will help you. We have moved to our other home, so you can move in immediately."

"Mom, there is not any water here. I wonder where we can get our water?" Howard said as he looked across the road to his new neighbors.

"Howard, I think we can get water from the neighbors," Annie said quickly, noticing worry in his voice.

"We have to have water. I will run across the road and see if we can get it from their well," Howard said aloud as he went out the door and across the road.

When the neighbor saw Howard, he hollered, "Hi neighbor. It's nice to meet you!"

"I'm pleased to meet you, too," Howard replied. "I have a favor to ask. Would it be possible for us to get our water supply from you?"

"Of course you can. Just help yourself whenever you need water."

"Thanks! Thanks a lot! That will surely be nice. Just knowing we will have a water supply is a lift off of my shoulders. I must be going if I want to get settled in with my family," Howard said as he crossed the road to go home.

"Well, Mom, at least we will have water and that is some relief. When there is a dry spell," he said, "we can get it from several different neighbors. They all know there is no water here. As a matter of fact, we need some now. Bobby, will you go get a pail of water? Go to the grocery store to get it. We will get our drinking water from there."

"But Daddy, that's over a block from here. Isn't that too far to carry water?"

"Yes, it is quite far to carry it, but Ethel, Viola, and the others will all take turns to get the water. For washing, we will get it closer to our place."

Their house was located in a small town called Harrisville. It was a lovely place with very friendly people. The population was approximately two hundred and fifty. This quiet little village was built among the hills and valleys in the Ohio Valley. It had tree-lined streets and sharp turns. The turns were so sharp that one passed directly in front of the same house three times to get down the hill.

"Now I know why they called this hill Three Bend Hill," Howard exclaimed. "There are three big turns just to get down this one hill. It's awesome. You pass directly in front of the same house three times. This landmark stands out to many people who drive through, and I can surely see why."

"This is surely an interesting place to live in. The people are all so nice. In a town of this size, it doesn't take long before you know every one who lives here," Howard exclaimed.

Poverty could be seen up and down the streets of this little country town. "With so many poor people, we fit right in," Howard told Annie. "I guess we have the largest family of them all though."

"Just being poor is not the worse thing that can happen to us. It is only bad because of so many extras to buy for. So our hardship presents more of a problem than the other families living here. It is a tossup which of us will survive if any of us do," Howard remarked.

On the night they moved in, the children were tucked into bed. Suddenly, they yelled, "Daddy! It's raining on our bed!" Hurriedly, Howard ran to their room. He pushed their bed to the side and put a bucket under the place where the water was coming from the roof. He had no idea the roof leaked or that it would rain that night. Before morning, he had to put buckets, pots, and pans everywhere to catch the water. " I have some tar left. Tomorrow I will put tar over the holes in the roof, and then it won't leak any more. The tar will help to keep the rain out," Howard told the children.

When morning came, Howard looked for the can of tar. "What did I do with it?" he said aloud. When he could not find it, he suddenly remembered he did not have any left. He had used it on another project. Even after weeks and months went by, there was still no money to buy the tar needed to cover the holes in the roof. Every time it rained Howard hollered, "Grab the pots and pans! We need them all. The blamed roof seems to be leaking everywhere. Hurry up! Get the pans before we are all swimming!"

While Howard was working vigorously, trying to add a couple rooms to this little three-room house, Mr. Herman appeared. Howard was working so fast to make more room for his large family he was not aware of his being present.

"You work much too hard, Howard. You had better slow down a bit if you want to live to see this project finished."

"Mr. Herman. I didn't hear you coming by. Yes, I am working a bit overtime. I have to get this finished before the snow flies."

"Do you think you can spare me a few hours work? I am getting behind, and I thought you maybe could use a bit more money."

"I certainly do need more money. Did you want me tonight?"

"No, no, tomorrow will be fine. I had some business to tend to in town, so I just dropped by to see if you could help me."

"Sure, I'll be there the first thing in the morning." Howard was always grateful for a little work. He stopped his own work and began to clean up the bits and pieces that were lying on the ground, so he could leave early to help him.

Howard was in such dire need for a little extra money. He was glad to have all the work he could get. He did not want to waste a minute. He wanted to get to Herman's early to get a long day's work in before dark. The story was always the same, never enough places to find a job, and never enough jobs to go around. He didn't want to take a chance and miss out on a day's work, so he made sure to please him to the best of his ability.

Mr. Herman was a kind, loving man, a truly caring man, and he tried to help make life a bit easier for Howard and his family in every small way he could.

While Howard was hard at work, Mr. Herman said, "Howard, I know you are trying to make your home bigger to have room for your family. Let's walk over to the barn. I have some old boards just lying around. I'm sure you could use them."

"You are so good to me, but you know I can't pay you for them. I can't pay you anything for the lumber because I don't have any money. Thanks anyway for your kindness, but I just can't keep taking things from you and not paying for them," was Howard's reply.

"Howard, please. Now you listen, I want to give these boards to you. I want to get them out of here and out of the way. What better way to get rid of an eyesore than to make good use of something?"

"Thanks, thank you so much. I sure need them bad. When I saw those boards, how I had wished I could buy them from you. Knowing I didn't have the money to pay for them, I hesitated to ask you for them. I can't get ahead no matter how hard I try. I guess what I'm trying to say is I don't want you to feel sorry for me. For sure I don't want to keep taking advantage of you. Mr. Herman, I'm so grateful, so very grateful to you! Thanks so much! I will work extra time to pay off the lumber."

"Now, now, Howard. Let's finish up the work, then we will get the lumber loaded. It won't take us long. It gets dark a little earlier now, but when we finish this job, we will load the lumber so you can get home. Maybe you will be able to get it unloaded before it gets dark."

"All right, Mr. Herman. I'll hurry this job up a bit. Then I'll get started on my way."

Howard had been working feverishly, spending many long hours to get the new addition added on to their small home before winter set in. He also wanted to get it finished before their new baby was due. Working at the task every minute he could, at long last, he had the job finished, much to his relief, and not any too soon.

"Mom, being our baby is due soon, in fact, any day now. I am so happy to have more room for our kids. Our meager little house is still too small, but it is much larger than before. It is home, Mom, and really, home is where I always want to be."

Annie tried to muster a smile. She wanted to keep an optimistic attitude and an upbeat mood, but no matter how hard she tried, she was losing a little of her quick wit. She was still happy with everything Howard did, and she trusted him. She could find very little fault with him, so she forced herself to smile. She wanted to change the hopeless feeling that had been so prominent these past months.

Thinking back to Howard's remark about being happy to have more room for their family, she said, "Howard who needs a palace? A home full of caring is what is important—caring for those around you. These walls will have to be strong to withstand so much of a good thing. I hope we have instilled this in our kids. We have done our best. Now I hope they all turn out good."

"Our home is one in a million, Annie, and you have been the one who made it this way," Howard said as they were discussing the new addition he had just finished on their house.

"Howard, I hate to interrupt your line of thought, but I am not feeling well. Maybe you should call Dr. McCleaster. I think I'm going into labor. Tell Viola she should gather the young ones and take them to Ruthie's house. Tell her to ask Ruthie to come and help get things ready for the delivery."

"OK, Mom. I'll hurry. I know I will be glad when this is all over."

"Viola!" Howard called. "Take the kids and go to Ruthie's. Tell her Mom is about to have our baby." Obediently, Viola took the younger children, so the house would be quiet when the baby made its entrance into the world.

The Love of Annie

Ruthie ran to Mom's side to help with the delivery and left her own home unattended. Her younger sisters and brothers would watch over her children, while she helped her mama get ready for the new baby's arrival.

The children were hungry and constantly went to the kitchen to get a bite of fried potatoes their sister had made for her own children. "Don't eat her potatoes," Viola said. "You kids can't eat those potatoes. Ruthie made them for their supper."

"OK, we won't eat them all. But they are so good," the youngsters told her.

The birth went quite smoothly. Dixie was the newest and the last arrival in the family. Howard was a bit shaken to see his Annie suffer again through another childbirth. He clasped her hand as he looked into her tired eyes.

"Ten children, Annie, and you are still the prettiest woman I have ever seen."

"You are just a little prejudiced, aren't you?"

"Maybe I am, Mom, but you have kept me from falling apart. You see, Mom, I have more than just you being pretty; I have you standing by me. I'm so glad this birth is over with. This is it, ten kids! As much as we love them, this is it!"

Annie didn't seem to have as much stamina after Dixie was born. Her energy level was gone. She was much more tired than when the other children were born.

Often when Howard came home, he would find Annie engrossed in her own thoughts. Trying to break her train of thought, he would slip his arm around her waist and dance a few steps. But it was beginning to get more difficult to get a hearty laugh from her, if any.

Annie became more and more quiet and withdrawn. She kept little Dixie close by her side. Often when Dixie cried, she did not hear her. She sat looking out of the window. The baby was so tired, wanting to be put into bed and needing other attention, but Annie did not realize it.

When the older children tried to put Dixie to bed, Annie quickly said, "No, no! Don't take her! Leave her right where she is."

Again and again, Elsie said, "Mama, can I put Dixie to bed? She is so tired, and she is crying."

"No, no! You leave her right there. I will take care of her," Annie answered. Night after night, Elsie begged to take care of little Dixie, and again and again, Annie refused to let any one pick her up. When the crying got loud enough, it shook Annie out of the trance she seemed to be in so much of the time and drew her attention to the baby. Then she lovingly took care of her little one. She did not realize she was neglecting Dixie Eileen.

Each time Annie became quiet, or lost interest in her surroundings, there was a little something that could bring her sweet, loving way back. Though her energy wavered back and forth, and depression dominated her life, there were times when she would be her old self again. Then Howard felt that his Annie would snap out of the terrible sadness and depression that hovered over her life so constantly.

These days, Howard felt the crunch more and more, since he had to watch over Annie more than usual. It was Annie who had been by Howard's side to encourage him and keep his spirits high. Now Howard had to be there to watch over his Annie. Yet, in their own way, each tried to keep their hopes high for a better tomorrow.

"Where does the time go?" Howard remarked one summer afternoon. "It is hard to believe time goes by so fast. I'm still trying to get over last year. I thought last year went fast. It is time to weed the garden. I'm counting on our garden to see us through these next few months. I would like you older ones to go down to Mr. Johnson's farm and hoe the weeds. He let me put a garden out there this year. The sun is already getting high, so it is going to be a scorcher. Go before it gets too hot. By mid-afternoon that sun is going to be mighty hot. If we don't get those weeds out, we won't get anything out of the garden, and heaven knows we need it," Howard told the children.

"OK," the children said. "Let's go! Two miles to the garden will take a lot of time to get there," Bobby announced.

It was already getting hot before they got on their way, and walking along the dusty road made them thirsty.

Mrs. Johnson, the farmer's wife, greeted them with a smile. "After you get a drink, come into my house. I have just made jelly, and I have fresh baked bread. You can have some to eat. I know kids all like to eat. Afterwards, you can weed a little in the garden."

Not having fresh bread and jelly at home, without any hesitation, they said OK. When they were through eating, she showed them the way to her garden. The children did not realize she had expected them to hoe her garden. Since they had eaten the bread and jelly, they felt obligated to do as they were told. But when they had finished, it was too late to do their own. They went home very tired and feeling bad that they didn't do their daddy's garden, as they were instructed.

In disbelief that anyone would have the gall to use bread and jelly to entice his children to do her work, made Howard angry. "Well, that . . . that conniving woman! How could anyone be that low to use food as a source for you to do her work? Well, I would say, that's pretty bad!"

"I'm sorry, Daddy," the children said almost in unison.

"Daddy, we didn't know we had to hoe her garden. We thought she was nice to give us some bread and jelly to eat. It sounded good, so we went in the house and ate it. We didn't know we wouldn't be able to get our garden done."

"I'm not blaming you kids. She knew what she was doing. Tomorrow, I will go along also. She took advantage of you. If this ever happens again, she will have to be set straight on the matter. Otherwise, just tell her you have to hoe our own garden, and it will be too late to do hers. I can't believe that she would be so low as to bribe you kids with food. She knew it would be too much of a temptation for you kids to resist. To think a grown woman could be so conniving with youngsters to offer bread and jelly and then tell them to hoe her garden in return. Oh well. What is done is done. Wash up, and get into bed now. We will go early in the morning, and we will get the garden done." As the children scampered off to bed Howard yelled, "Goodnight. I will see you in the morning. And don't forget to say your prayers."

Chapter 18

Up early the next morning, Howard and the children went to the garden and were through with the hoeing sooner than expected. On the way home, he decided the children should have some time off to do what they wanted.

"Bobby, since we left our farm, you are so restless. Why don't you and one of the others go to visit Ruthie today? Do you know how to get there?"

"Yes, Daddy, I think so."

"Are you sure you know the way? I want you to get there safely. Well, just remember, you go down the road apiece, then you go straight around the corner. You go down the road apiece further, then you go straight around that corner right into Ruthie's farm yard. It is hot out, so don't you kids toy along the way."

"OK, Daddy, we won't stay too long. Come on Gladys. She has a current patch. We will pick some currants. Let's go see her, OK?" It was a hot humid day, but with Bobby's

~ **The Love of Annie**

determination, once he made up his mind he wanted to do something, you could not change his mind. "Come on now Gladys. Let's go!"

"OK," Gladys answered, "I'll go with you."

"Just see that you are back before it gets dark," Howard hollered as they started on their way.

On each bend in the road, Bobby said, "Let's go this way. If we go straight across the turn in the road, it will be closer." Gladys believed everything her brother said, so she followed his every step. By the time they crossed each turn in the road, thinking it would save steps. Their feet and legs were too tired to even think of picking currants.

A few steps were saved on some turns, but the constant going back and forth was much worse then following the road.

Ruthie smiled when she saw how tired they were. "When you go home, just follow the road. It will be much closer and easier on your legs. Crossing back and forth is not closer, so just go straight around the turns in the road. Crossing the turns doesn't save you many steps."

The two thought it was fun and wanted to go to their sister's house again the next day.

"Don't you remember what I told you?" Howard quickly said. "'Where they want you lots, go little; where they want you little, go not at all.' You can't pester people too often. Ruthie will never say anything, but it is better to space your visits further apart."

"But Daddy, she said she wants us to come back."

"I'm sure she did tell you that, and I know she meant it. But you have to give her family a little privacy too, you know."

"OK, Daddy. We won't go for two more days."

"I think you mean two more months, don't you?"

"No, Dad. I think a couple of days would give them enough of . . . of . . . what's that word you said?"

"Privacy. Plain speaking, it means you should stay home for awhile so they can be alone."

"I sure wouldn't want to be alone, would you, Gladys?"

"No, I want to be with you, Bobby."

"Well, anyway, you can't go to see Ruthie again for awhile," Howard told them very firmly. "We will talk about it when the time comes. Don't you kids have something to do about now?"

"I guess so. Come on, Gladys. Let's find some kids and play ball." Out they went without another word.

Summer passed into fall so quickly, and a crisp chill was in the air. Halloween night was a favorite night in Howard and Annie's home. The town children made their rounds and stopped at different places to pick up a little candy. The kids loved to play tricks on Howard and Annie, because they got right into the act, also, throwing corn or whatever.

As Howard and Annie watched through the window, they could see the kids coming long before they realized they were being watched. As the children came nearer to the house, corn hit the windows with a zing and a thud. Then there were knocks, first at the door, then at the windows. Then more corn was thrown, and the kids hollered and laughed.

Annie said, "Howard, let's surprise them. There is a bucket of tomatoes in the corner in the kitchen. I didn't feel up to canning them, and they are getting a little mushy. Let's toss a few tomatoes lightly at the kids."

When they opened the door, zing! Tomatoes flew at Howard and Annie, just missing Howard's head.

~~ **The Love of Annie**

Laughing, he said, "It takes a better pitch than that. You missed!" No sooner had he said that than the next one caught him square on his forehead. He laughed so hard. The kids out threw Howard and Annie, two to one. They didn't think the town kids would have the same idea as they, throwing tomatoes on Halloween night.

The element of surprise gave the kids the advantage in the tomato throwing. When Howard and Annie started throwing tomatoes back at the kids, it gave them the action they were looking for. Tomatoes flew back and forth, with Annie and Howard laughing as hard and loud as the kids did. When the tomatoes were gone, the children left as quickly as they had come. Everyone felt the happiness of this night.

After Halloween, a few of the young people began to drop in regularly. "They seem to feel right at home," Annie remarked to Howard. "With so many children of all ages, we will soon have the whole town dropping in."

Annie loved it and showed signs of getting back to her old self. . . . at least, a little more than she had been for some time. This seemed to take her mind off herself and their problems. It didn't take long before all the young people gathered at their home.

Howard built a big porch on the side of their house. Close by was a huge oak tree. He decided to put a strong cable on one of the huge limbs on the tree and make a swing for the children to have something to play on. He fastened an old tire to the end of the cable, and the swing was ready to go. How they loved it because the porch that Howard had built was the perfect place and height for the kids to swing from. It took one person to hand the swing up to the one next in line for their turn to swing. Their laughter told

The Love of Annie

how much fun they had. The porch was so high, the swing went down to the ground before lifting them up into the air. The children's heads would touch the small limbs of the tree. The height it went into the air inevitably brought a loud scream. The children waiting in line for their turn enjoyed watching the others swing. Children, from the better-off families to the utmost poorest, met here daily.

As time went by each one had his or her own reason for meeting at this most humble home. Some had a secret crush on one of the others who met there, while others came to go sled riding or take a short walk up the street to a small lunch room. The porch became a meeting place of all ages with such fun and laughing every night. People found someone or something to fill their evening when they met at this home.

Telling ghost stories often became a whole evening of entertainment. Since one of the farm homes Howard's family lived in was said to be haunted, it was a tossup as to who would tell their story first. When the stories were all told, some children were afraid to go home. With so many kids all adding their own gory details, it made each story even more scary. But there were enough children going the same direction, so it didn't present too much of a problem.

As if this wasn't scary enough, the radio was a source of fun and entertainment. The ghost stories on *Inner Sanctum* sometimes took precedence over others. Every night, kids would come back and sit on or around the little front porch of this very old, but love-filled, home. There was enough love in this home for the whole town to share.

"The kids showed up early today," Howard remarked one day as he watched them waiting to take their turns on the big swing. After awhile one of them said, "Let's play hide-and-seek for awhile." Quickly they jumped from the porch and started their game.

Way back in the shadows, beneath the old porch, was the perfect hiding place. As one boy scampered back into the darkness, he sat on something a little unfamiliar. Wondering what had made a crackling sound, he put his hand beneath him to see what he was sitting on. He soon discovered what it was. He had sat on a nest of eggs.

Our neighbor's chickens had found it a perfect place to lay their eggs. Not wanting to be caught or to give up his hiding place, the boy sat quietly. Soon these eggs were well scrambled. He tried to hide the yellow yokes on the seat of his pants, but inevitably someone noticed. The boy mustered a smile and said, "I just scrambled them quicker and a lot better." It didn't take much to get a laugh or a joke out of these kids, especially when the joke was on someone else.

These young people referred to this humble home as "Town Hall," or "Bright Corner," whichever name they chose to call it when they talked about meeting there. Annie and Howard loved it.

"Mom, I would much rather have our kids sitting at home than running around and walking the streets at night. At least we know where they are and what they are doing," Howard remarked.

"They will also stay out of trouble this way. Besides, I love those kids," Annie replied.

"They are all good kids. Funny, we are so poor, but that doesn't make any difference. They still love to come here." Of course, Howard was never one to be out done. When one of them played a joke on him, he decided to play one back. Often, when the front porch was lined with the young people having their usual good time, Howard would make some chocolate candy. When no one was looking, he'd put castor oil in it. After several times, they caught on to Howard's joke and were on the lookout for some way to get back at him. They never ceased to surprise Howard, and they kept coming back for more.

Often they would say, "Sparky, do you have any more of that good candy?"

His reply was, "No, but I will make some," and he'd proceed to do so. The kids gave Howard the name "Sparky" because he had an old mule that was used in the coal mine. The mule was so stubborn, he would not budge. Over and over again, they had tried to get the mule to pull and work with the coal, but he just balked, so the boss said, "Howard, do you want a mule?"

"Sure, I'll take him," Howard answered.

"Well, I surely hope you have better luck with him than we are having."

Howard, being a soft-spoken man, only had to work with the mule for a short time. The mule did not like to climb a certain hill, but with kind words Howard could get the mule to do anything. The mule would balk a little and then go. "You just have to be patient with him," Howard said. "The people who worked with the mule in the coal mines would swear and holler at him. He is just like people. You can get someone to do more for you with kindness than being mean."

There was a talking parrot on this hill that belonged to a neighbor, Ori Donley. This parrot constantly hollered, "Polly want a cracker! Polly want a cracker!" The mule would look at the parrot, then very slowly move on. When the children thought the parrot said a swear word, Howard would say, "Now you kids had better listen a bit more closely. That parrot don't swear."

The kids loved watching Howard work with the mule. It was hilarious, so the teasing began. They began to call Howard "Sparky." This added more enjoyment to Howard's life. This loving nickname stuck with Howard the rest of his life—long after the old mule was gone. Simple pleasure was his life, and everyone loved him for it, including his Annie.

Chapter 19

Election Day was upon them, and in this election year, people hoped times might get better for every one with a new administration running for office.

No one, except a handful of the luckier ones, had anything. Money was always scarce, and there were many little feet to buy shoes for and many mouths to feed. Again, there was never enough to pay the bills. They were lucky to keep Howard's carbide light working and in shape for what few days of work he had. The mines were so dark, men had to use a light to pick the coal from the vein that ran beneath the ground.

The miners were glad when they had a day's work at the mines, so they never complained of the bad conditions. Since they were striking so much of the time, and the picketers were going by constantly, it was quite a worry. The fear that strikers would get angry and take their anger out on others weighed heavily on Howard's mind.

If Howard and the children were sitting on the porch when strikers drove back and forth, Howard, wanting to protect the children, made them duck behind his chair. It was frightening to think that some of the picketers might throw rocks if they thought someone was crossing the picket line. He was fearful for the children's safety. "Get behind our chairs. Hurry up! Duck down so they won't see you as they drive past," Howard said quickly. The children would hide until told to come out. "They are gone now; the picketers are gone. They are out of sight. You can get out from behind the chairs now. They are not going to hurt anyone; they kept going."

"Daddy, they are gone. Help me put a piece of cardboard in my shoes. My feet are cold. It feels good when you fix my shoes. It stays better than when I do it," one child remarked.

"Yes, honey. The cardboard is stiffer, so it does stay in better than paper does."

"But, Daddy, I couldn't find any cardboard."

"I know, honey. Sometimes we don't have any to put in your shoes, but I fixed them. Now your feet will be toasty warm."

"Your daddy is smart. He can fix anything," Annie chimed in.

Fall was turning into winter. It was getting cold and bitter outside. "Viola! Viola," a neighbor called from across the street. "Will you run to the store for me? I need bread and milk for dinner."

"Yes, I'll get it for you," Viola hollered as she crossed the street to get the money. Annie flinched as though she was thinking, *Don't ask her to go out in this bitter cold.* But she didn't tell her not to go.

The Love of Annie

The one whose name was called would go quickly to run the errand for her. Usually it was Viola, but on occasion, Ethel or Gladys was called. The children had been taught very diligently to treat others exactly the way they would want others to treat them. If someone needed help, they were taught to do as they were asked.

One bitter winter day, when the neighbor hollered, the youngest one of the three girls went on the errand. "Would you go to the grocery store and get me a quart of milk?" the neighbor asked. Obediently she went on her way. The soles of her shoes were so badly worn, however, that the cardboard no longer stayed in the shoes. She thought it would be much easier to go barefoot, though there was snow on the ground. So off she trotted to buy the milk, without any shoes on her feet.

As she was running to the store, a neighbor lady called out, "Honey, come here for a minute." She obeyed her command and hurried to see what she wanted. "Here, you wear this pair of shoes. You can't go clear uptown with no shoes on your feet. Please wear this pair of mine," Mrs. Anthony said.

"No, no," she said. "I'm not cold." The neighbor lady would not listen. She insisted that she wear her shoes the rest of the way.

Trying not to admit she was cold, the little one repeated, "I'm not cold. I run fast. I run real fast. I won't get cold." The neighbor lady would not give up. So at her insistence, she finally gave in and wore her shoes.

On her way home, she stopped to give the shoes back to the lady, gave the neighbor her milk, and hurried home to get warm.

Everyone was finding it more difficult to make ends meet. People everywhere were feeling the crunch of the Great Depression. It was truly a disaster. You had only to look around; the signs of the times were evident—people everywhere were devastated at our country's situation. Automobiles were more plentiful, but money was scarce. Many could not afford to buy gasoline for the car. People walked to where they were going most of the time.

Entertainment for most was playing dominoes or a game of cards. Children entertained themselves. They didn't have the pleasures of today. The young people would meet on a corner and play hide-and-seek; run, sheepy, run; kick-the-can; Andy, Andy, over; play ball; or a game that most children loved, marbles. The ones who could shoot a marble the best ended up with the most marbles. "We will play marbles for keeps," the kids would say before the game started, so each knew the best shooter would go home with the most marbles. Children entertained themselves.

There were no televisions to entertain them. When they went to school, they went to learn reading, writing, and arithmetic. There were no busses to haul children to another town or city for a sports competition of any kind. That was unheard of in those days.

Poor Annie did not even own a dishcloth or a dishtowel. Once they were worn, there was no money to buy anymore. There was absolutely no money for such a luxury as a dishtowel or dishcloth. She didn't have even a washcloth or bath towel any longer. There was not a thread of a towel to be used. What clothes could be worn at all had to be used for that purpose only. When a dress, or an apron, or any piece of clothing, was worn to the point of no repair, it would be washed clean and torn and used to wash and dry the dishes or to use for bathing.

The life of Annie was not good. There was not enough food, not enough clothing, not enough money to pay the bills, and she could no longer buy pink ribbon to tie in her hair or the material to make the white aprons she loved so much. As was the case so often, she had barely enough to exist.

What Annie really wanted was very little. There was a certain face soap, which she liked better than the other brands. This particular soap was a penny or two higher in price than the other brands of soap. One day when she needed soap, she called Anna Lee and asked if she would please run to the store and get a bar. "Tell them I would like a bar of this brand of soap, will you please?"

"Yes, Mama, I will get you the soap."

The owner of the store asked Anna Lee, "Could I help you with something today?"

"Yes, Mama wants a bar of soap. She asked me to buy her a certain kind of soap and to be sure to ask for that kind. Now I am mixed up what kind she wanted. Do you know what kind of soap Mama would want?"

"Yes, she uses this kind, but I will send her a bar of this other soap. This brand is cheaper. Tell your mother this is just as good for your skin as any of the other brands are. Tell her she should try this. I'm sure she will like it if she tries it once."

Not receiving the soap she wanted upset Annie. Seldom did she show how she felt, but not being able to even buy her favorite soap made her sad. She was more depressed than ever and began to feel unworthy and a little bitter.

~≈ **The Love of Annie**

Things are getting way out of hand, Annie thought. For a while, she felt angry but then realized there was nothing she could do about it. She finally accepted the inevitable, thinking she was probably lucky to have any soap at all.

Winter arrived, and it was a severe one. The wind howled and whistled around the house. It gave an eerie feeling, knowing the cold that goes with it would soon be badly felt because they had no money to buy coal. Annie walked back and forth through the house, wondering how they could keep the house warm enough to get through the day. She shivered as she tried to decide what to do. While thinking about the situation, little Billy came in and yelled, "Look, Mama, I found some coal."

"Where did you find it, Billy?"

"I dug it out of the ash pile. See Mama, it all didn't burn up. It will keep us warm."

"Oh, thanks, pet. Thank you. This will keep us warm for awhile."

The next day was the same—bitter and cold—and still they had no coal. "Bobby, would you go to Milt"s and borrow a bucket of coal? We will pay him back." Bobby went to get the coal. When he asked to borrow it, Milt knew they needed it badly, so he filled the bucket with as much as he thought he could carry. He knew he would not get the coal back—at least, not very soon, if at all.

Every so often, Billy or one of the others would dig in the ash pile to find a small bit of coal that didn't quite burn up. When the cold nights of winter hit, there were not enough quilts or blankets to cover the children. The Great Depression had lasted much too long already. What bedding they had was not enough for everyone to be warm. "What can I cover up with? I'm cold!" cried one of the children.

"Now, now, honey, we will cover you up so you can be nice and warm. There, there, now you will be warm," Annie said as she covered the little one up with coats. To keep warm, the coats they wore daily were also used to cover the children as they slept. Howard and Annie had to resort to anything to protect their children from the cold.

No matter how bad the daytime had been, when evening came and they were ready for bed, the children still happily knelt by Mama's knee and said their prayers. They didn't think about being poor. They were taught to accept whatever the circumstances were. They did not know each day was a challenge, just to have enough to eat. The whole country was trying to find ways to get by one day at a time. People did not go around complaining. They knew things could not be any better at this point. The depression was bad, very bad.

When Annie was deep in thought one day, a little neighbor girl asked, "Mrs. DeVault, can we borrow a cup of sugar? We will pay it back as soon as we can."

"Yes, I think I have enough left. Let me take a quick look. Yes, honey, I can spare you a cup today. I didn't hear you come in. I'm sorry, with the children being so noisy, I didn't hear the door open," Annie said.

"We will pay it back as soon as we can get some more," the little girl told Annie.

"That's OK. I need some flour. Do you think we could get a cup from your mother? I don't have enough to make biscuits for supper."

"I'll ask my mother if she has some you can borrow. Then I will tell you if she has any she can spare. It is nice we live so close to you, Mrs. DeVault. We can talk together from our porch."

~≈ The Love of Annie

"Yes, it's nice to have close neighbors. I like having someone near. I will send one of the children down with a cup. If your mother has an extra cup of flour to spare, it would sure help out a lot." Annie was happy to know she could get some; now she could get on with making supper. The main things they needed to borrow were sugar, salt, flour, baking powder, and lard; the main items needed to make pancakes or biscuits. Enough to feed the children, so they could do the necessary things that had to be done. And, so they would not go to school on an empty stomach.

It was nearly time for school to dismiss the next day when the teacher called the students to come to the front of the room. "Gladys, she said, "would you please remain sitting in your seat?" Wondering why everyone in the class was called except her, made her feel bad, as she sat alone at her desk near the back of the room, thinking the teacher didn't like her. There was no explanation as to why the others were picked, and she was not. The teacher meant only to make her happy. Being a little girl, she didn't understand why she was asked to remain sitting. Instead of making her happy, she felt left out and began to cry.

The next morning the teacher brought a small package and gave it to her in front of the class. "Here is a little present for you from all of your friends. I called them to the front of the room yesterday and asked each one to ask their parents if they could bring one penny to school. Each of them brought one penny, so we could buy you this little present." As Gladys slowly opened the package her hands shook from the excitement of what was inside. She could hardly open it fast enough. Inside of the package was a pair of black stockings.

"Your friends want you to be warm like they are, so each one brought one penny to buy these. We hope they will keep your feet nice and warm." Gladys mustered a smile and a meek thank you as the school bell rang.

The children scurried out of the classroom. Gladys followed behind slowly, still not understanding exactly what had taken place. No one seemed to notice the insecurity of this little girl at this tender young age.

The news got around about the classmates buying the stockings for her, and a well-meaning, quite wealthy family, bought nice dresses and other clothing for the family to wear. At first Annie was very appreciative, thinking tomorrow would be better. *Yes*, she thought, *tomorrow will be better. It has to be better. The sun will come out tomorrow.* Nothing seemed to change much though. Every day was worse then the day before.

When a birthday rolled around—no matter whose—it was just another day. There was never a birthday cake or a party. The day passed by as every other day. No one mentioned the special day at all. Perhaps someone would wish a happy birthday, but that was the extent of it. There was not a chance of getting a present from anyone on a birthday, not even a birthday cake or a card.

One morning, Howard awoke quite early. Something was weighing on his mind. "Mom," he said, "next Sunday is Easter morning. How are we going to handle it? We have barely enough in the house to eat now. I know the gift of the Resurrection is the utmost important thing about Easter, and I'm sure we have instilled this in our kids. It seems the whole world is so wrapped up in the candy bit and the Easter Bunny. I sometimes wonder if it hurts them to see other kids get candy when they don't."

"Howard, we have never talked to the children of candy and good things to eat. We have taught our kids that God will supply our every need. And Howard they won't make a big issue of it if we treat Easter day for what it really is—a day of rejoicing that Jesus has risen from the dead. Resurrection Day! Howard, if one should ask why the Easter Bunny didn't come, we will tell them the truth. There are children everywhere. There are so many children in the world, and a lot of children will not be able to get candy this year. We have good understanding kids, Howard. They will probably not even think of being left out, so don't fret. We will get them through the day, I'm sure. When they are wide awake and we attend the church service, it will give them better things to think about."

As Easter Sunday approached no more was said about the Easter Bunny. It was a beautiful morning; the sun was so warm and bright. One by one the children headed for the warmth on the front porch. Not once did they feel neglected or poor.

Everyone was out early enjoying this beautiful day. As Iona, a young neighbor girl, walked by she hollered across the street, "What did the Easter Bunny bring you?"

" Nussin," one of the little ones replied as they all went about their childish play.

" Didn't the Easter Bunny bring you some candy?"

"No, he had too many kids to see."

"Didn't he bring you any candy at all?"

"No, nussin. He has too many places to go."

About that time, they heard an excited little girl scream with delight. She lived in the house close by. When they jumped up from their play to see what her excitement was about, they saw a huge white rabbit hanging on her doorknob and a big basket of candy sitting below it. The little girl grabbed the bunny with sheer delight, took the basket, and hurriedly went back into her house. As these children watched her disappear through the front door, they thought only that the Easter Bunny found her. Only a few remarks were made about the little girl being so happy with what the Easter Bunny had brought her. They didn't question why she had so much and they had none.

"You see, Howard," Annie said, "they need only to feel how much we care for them, and the true meaning of Easter. After church service, and after we have a bite to eat, we will play games with them. They all enjoy dominoes. We will get the dominoes out later on this afternoon. With the crate of eggs my boss gave us, the kids can see who can eat the most eggs. That should be fun to watch them."

"One thing, Mom, as summer comes, things are usually a little better. We will plan our Fourth of July picnic at the Webster schoolhouse. We can plan for that real soon. I love the excitement I see in their faces at the thought of the bologna sandwiches. And, Mom, how I love to watch them as they keep going back and forth to the tub of watermelon in cold water until we finish with the rest of the picnic. I hope we can do it this year again. That's one day the children look forward to. Johnny is working now and will help out with some of the food. He helps us so much," Howard remarked.

"Yes, I know," Annie answered. "That boy is a blessing to have around. I don't know what we would have done without him."

The remaining weeks before the Fourth of July picnic went quickly. With Johnny's help, it was such a happy day. Though everything else seemed to remain the same—the day still was a happy one.

Summer was full of happy days. Howard taught each of his children how to swim. He took each child on his back while in the old swimming hole at Foxes Bottom. After swimming around awhile, he ducked under the water. They learned quickly to hold their nose and not be afraid of water. When he promised to take Gladys and her friend, Alice, swimming, he did so although he had seven flat tires in less than three miles. Without a word of discouragement, he patiently patched the inner tube each time, and at long last reached the Foxes Bottom creek.

As fall was approaching, Annie became sadder and more depressed than usual. No longer was there a happy smile or a twinkle in her beautiful brown eyes. She cried more and more often. This saddened Howard. "Oh God, dear God, if I could only have one penny to rub against the other one." Things were out of his control.

"Where do I go for help? We are already on relief. I guess I had better not complain. They give us prunes, grapefruit, and corn meal. At least it's something to put on the table. It helps for a few days anyway," Howard said aloud.

A few days later, when a little neighbor girl came over to play, she was eating a slice of bread and peanut butter. It looked so good to the kids, especially to the smaller ones, because there was nothing that good in their own home to eat. One of the youngsters asked, "Can we have some of that too, Daddy? Can we buy some bread and peanut butter?"

This was too much for Howard. He brushed away the tears as he hurried out the door. Knowing he had no money to buy the bread and peanut butter, he left the room, so he would not have to answer a question that literally broke his heart and tore him to pieces.

The children never complained. They took their life as it was, not knowing the anguish and worries their mama and daddy were experiencing. No one talked about it. No one ever said, "You are poor. You don't have anything." Howard and Annie lived one day at a time and tried exceptionally hard to raise their children in this manner. They never questioned the whys in their life: why they did not have this or that, or why others had things they did not have. To them, loving and caring for each other and those around them were the necessary things they needed in life. The thought of comparing their lives to what others had or did not have never occurred to them.

At the end of summer, Billy decided to see if the neighbor's chickens were still laying eggs under the old porch. He crawled back to the corner, where the boy had sat on the pile of eggs. To his happy surprise, those chickens had not let him down. He found a nest of eggs, gathered the eggs in his little hands, and took them into the house, hoping Mama would fry them for dinner. As Annie dropped her head and stood quietly for what seemed a long time, Billy said, "Mama can you fry these eggs for us?"

Mama felt her heart ache as she looked down into his little face, so full of anticipation of eating a fried egg. Finally, she said, "Yes, Billy, I will fry these eggs, but soon I want to tell you something."

As Annie prepared the eggs, she had a look of concern on her face, yet a little quirk of a smile was in the corner of her mouth. After they were through eating, Annie waited until the other children had gone out to play before approaching Billy about the eggs.

She called Billy to her side. "Billy, would you please come here for a minute? I want to tell you something."

"Just a minute, Mama. I want to be by you alone. I'll close the door so the other kids won't know what you are going to tell me." Acting a little smug at the thought that he alone was getting all of this attention and he did not have to share it with any one else, Billy closed the door and went back to where his mama was waiting. Annie went to Billy's side and drew him close to her breast.

"Billy, those eggs were so good. As I watched your little face I knew you had your mind set on how good they were going to taste. I felt I could not take that away from you, so that is the reason I fried them, pet. We know they were not really our eggs. We know they belong to our neighbor. But this can be our secret, just between you and me forever?"

"Ok, Mama, I won't tell. This is our secret, Mama."

"Yes, pet, but I have to tell you something else. When you find more eggs, we will have to take them to John. They are his chickens, so the eggs belong to him. Promise me you will take the eggs to him if you find anymore."

"I will, Mama. I will take the eggs back to him."

"That's my boy. It is the right thing to do, you know. This is the first secret we have had together, so don't tell a soul. Remember, this is just between you and me. Now go play, and remember what to do when you find more eggs."

"I'll take them to John." Billy went to find more eggs, so he could keep this little secret with Mama till the end. He was thinking as he scampered out the door, *I've got a secret with Mama, and I can't tell anyone else!* He knew he would keep this secret forever.

Howard noticed Annie was keeping to herself more than usual. Often when he came home, Annie did not know he was around, and he would see her crying. This hurt Howard. *Mom, poor, poor, Mom,* he said to himself. He could not hide his fears much longer. He knew Annie was about to break. She had tried for much too long to be the strong one, to keep Howard from giving up, but now she was showing signs of terrible strain.

Dixie was home, and the others were in school. The change in Annie was noticeable. Menopause alone was more than enough for any woman with such stress as Annie had. Nervousness and the fear of what the future held showed in her disposition, where in the past she was always smiling and happy. Now with the future bleak and all her hopes and dreams shattered, she seemed to find little to smile about, though she hid her feelings quite well.

"Mama," Johnny said, "my girlfriend Margaret and I are getting married. I love her so much. We'll live in Georgetown. It's only three miles in case you need me."

"If this is what you want, it has to be your decision. I had hoped you would wait until you were a bit older, but I'm sure you know what you are doing. I hope you will be happy, and I am glad you will be living close to us. We will like having you near," was his mama's reply.

Chapter 20

Chaos was just around the corner. Anna Lee had a sharp pain behind her ear, and it was almost more then she could stand. When the doctor came, he knew immediately it was mastoids. "We have to relieve the pressure quickly," he said. "Get some blankets and spread them out on the table." They spread the blankets out smoothly, put Anna Lee gently on the table, and began the surgery. The children were sent out, so it would be quiet while he operated. They stood by the house, quietly waiting to see if their sister was going to be OK.

The children didn't understand what was going on, since there was no time for an explanation. Hearing their sister's screaming from the pain, they stood frozen. The children thought she was dying and barely whispered their fears to each other.

At last it was over. "Anna Lee will be OK," the doctor announced. "You can go in to see her."

They yelled with excitement as they ran to the door.

"Hey! Hey, there!" the doctor hollered, trying to slow them down a little. "You must be quiet. She needs a lot of rest."

"We will be quiet. Can we go in to see her?"

"You can go in, but only to tell her you are glad she is going to be all right, then you must let her rest."

"We will. We will let her rest. Can we see her now?"

"Yes, but please stay only a few minutes. Now run along. She is tired, and she will probably fall asleep in a few minutes. That was quite an ordeal she went through."

The children tiptoed into where Anna Lee was lying. Her eyes were closed from sheer exhaustion, and she was much too tired to talk. When Billy realized she was going to be all right, her brother said with an ornery grin, "Now I know I can beat you in a race." Anna Lee was too tired to give him an argument. She only smiled a little.

As the doctor was leaving, Howard said, "Doctor, I can't pay you, but I will go to the bank tomorrow."

"Well, Howard. Will you be putting it in, or are you taking it out?" the good doctor asked.

"I'm afraid I will be taking it out. I don't have any money to pay you," Howard answered.

"That's hard on your assets," the doctor said as he left. Howard knew the doctor was trying to cheer him up. This extra worry did not help Annie's situation any. It only added more stress. Although Howard tried to make it easy for his Annie, there was nothing he could do. Every week seemed to present a different problem. They could only meet each stressful situation head on.

Annie was aware of things that could harm her family. But she was quite surprised when the children told her one morning that a bum had quietly opened the front door while the children were sleeping on a davenport. He came in, stoked up the fire in the potbellied stove, and then sat on the bed in front of one of the girls' face. After warming, himself, he left as quietly as he had come.

"Did he say anything to you, or did he touch any of you?"

"No, Mama. He just got warm, and then he went out again."

"Were you afraid of him?"

"A little bit, but we acted like we were asleep, Mama."

"Well, it is good to know that you are all OK. Most bums just want a little food or to get out of the cold and warm up a little. Then they go on their way again."

"Is that why these men stop here, Mama?"

"Yes, honey. I try to give them a bite to eat if I have anything to give them. They depend upon people to help them along the way."

The girls slept on a davenport that opened into a bed. Since the house was small and there were not enough beds to go around, two girls slept at the head of the bed, and two others at the bottom. Clothes were as scarce as the beds, and when someone gave Annie clothing or toys, she truly appreciated them. The clothes were used immediately, but the toys were hidden in a closet for Christmas presents.

"Elsie, you are the oldest child at home, so I will need a lot of help from you," Annie announced one day.

"I'll try to help you as much as I can, Mama," Elsie answered.

"I want you to stay home tonight. You can't go anywhere now. There are other things you can do," Annie told her, when a friend stopped by. Being an understanding girl, she obeyed her mama and stayed home. Each time someone asked her to go somewhere, the answer was the same.

The Love of Annie

"No, Elsie, you had better stay home tonight." Annie began to be very protective of her, and she was very stern about what Elsie could or could not do, particularly what she could not do. She was not allowed to date young men or go with her girl friends anywhere. For some reason, Annie had developed an irrational fear that someone was going to kidnap her and sell her for slavery.

Not understanding Annie's way of thinking, Howard tried to dispel this thought, but it didn't seem to help.

"Howard," Annie said, "you can't be too careful. Elsie is still young. She will have plenty of time to do what she wants to do when she is out of school and a mite older."

"I know, Mom, but she needs some time for herself. All young people need time for enjoyment."

After that, Annie watched Elsie even more closely than before. Howard tried to find a way to convince Annie to relent a little, but Annie never wavered. Howard knew Elsie should be having fun like the other young people, but he couldn't do anything to help her.

This abnormal thinking that Elsie would be kidnapped made Annie's life unhappy. Annie's grandparents had slaves, and although they had treated their slaves as their own family, it bothered Annie that slaves had been treated badly in other homes.

"Perhaps the worry Annie has of Elsie being kidnapped and sold, stems from when Annie's grandparents had these slaves," the doctor told Howard. "I'm sure Annie's mother grew up with a lot of questions about her own life and her children's lives. Also, Howard, you often talked of the horrendous fear Annie's mother displayed. When Annie was a child, you said she watched her closely and shaved her head bald. That tells a lot, Howard. Annie's mother grew up thinking if slaves could be taken from their homes, then perhaps something bad could happen to her children, too. As a result, she watched her own children too closely. What I'm trying to tell you, Howard, is that the treatment Annie received from her mother is perhaps what is causing her to be so overly protective of Elsie. You also told me how Annie had been pressured into a marriage she did not really want. Perhaps she was trying to make sure this didn't happen to her children. Don't worry. Eventually she will get over this. It is her other behavior that worries me more. Perhaps the ugliness of her past is making its mark on Annie these many years later," the doctor explained.

Annie had been burning Elsie's clothes, and since she had so few clothes anyway, it broke her heart to see her mother burn the few things that she did have. Whenever she got something new to wear, Annie would inevitably burn it. When she was about to throw her clothes in the potbellied stove, Elsie cried, "Mama, please don't burn my clothes! That's all I have to wear, Mama, please! Please don't burn them! Oh, Mama, I need them!" None of this stopped Annie, however. As usual, she opened the door on the potbellied stove and threw the clothes into the hot fire. Elsie cried, not knowing how hard her mother was struggling to keep herself from falling apart completely.

At this time, there was very little known about mental illness or what to do for a patient. Since doctors did not understand it well, the medicine they used did not help Annie. So instead of poor Annie getting the help she needed, the drug barely kept her mind intact and sane enough for her to stay at home with her loved ones.

On occasions, a well-to-do family gave a few new dresses to the younger girls also, but they never wore them. They were red and blue-flowered. The girls thought they were beautiful. For some peculiar reason, however, red seemed to set Annie off, so the dresses disappeared. Perhaps they were burned also. In any event, the girls never wore the dresses or even saw them again. Yet not once did they ask where the pretty dresses had gone. As usual, they took life as it was, with no questions.

Annie truly appreciated gifts from people, until she was too sick to realize how kind and well-meaning these people really were.

The fact that the new clothes were gone did not seem to bother the girls. They saw the dresses when they were brought to their home, but that was the last they were seen. The girls didn't have a chance to wear them—not once. Not even to school.

School days are said to be happy days, but Bobby didn't think so. Though he was very capable in every thing he did, he disliked school. In fact, he hated it and would do anything to keep from going. He loved the woods and fields that surrounded this small town and would often play hooky and go there instead of to school.

When Howard called, "Rise and shine kids. School starts today," Bobby pretended not to hear him. Howard hollered up the stairs, "Get out of bed! Do you hear me?"

"OK, OK, we are coming," one hollered back.

"I don't hear any movement up there," Howard said, as he started his favorite song.

> School days, school days, happy, happy school days.
> They have reading and writing, and you'll learn how to spell.
> Arithmetic I'm sure, and grammar as well.

Now get up and get dressed, today is the date.
It's the first day of school, so you must not be late.

Howard loved music and this was one of his favorite songs. Howard used this cheery verse to wake the kids in the morning. By the time he finished the song, the children were wide-awake.

Of course, Bobby was never happy when that day came. Until he was called by name, he didn't budge. With his daddy's type of humor, he hardly had a choice but to get up and go. But often where he ended up was in the woods, instead of at school. One day when he played hooky from school, a skunk was meandering along about that time. Bobby got too close to the skunk, or it got too close to him. He got sprayed, so he took off his pants, dug a hole, and buried them. Realizing he had no pants to wear to school, he hurriedly went back and dug them up again.

How Bobby wished he were older like Elsie, thinking then he would get out of school, also. He knew his sister was nearly through high school, and he didn't plan on going there. He thought in a short time, he, too, could do what he wanted, instead of wasting his time in a classroom.

All too soon, Elsie's high school days were coming to an end. Young men were becoming interested in her. She was getting invitations, but she could never go. She was at the age when her friends were going with boyfriends and running around, and she could not. It hurt her to be left out of things. She was young, and not realizing her mother was ill, she became upset. Having so few clothes, no chance to do the things her girl friends did, or just to be with her friends once in awhile, was very frustrating.

~≼ The Love of Annie

"Elsie," a neighbor said, "I can use someone to help me with my housework. Do you think you could work for me a little?"

"Yes, I can help you, Mrs. Thomas, but I have to bring my little sister with me because Mama is sick. Would that be all right?"

"Yes, of course, that will be fine. Bring the little one with you."

"Mama can't take care of her, but I will work hard for you."

"Don't worry, honey. You will do fine," Mrs. Thomas told Elsie. "We will get what is needed to be done out of the way today. You are still in school, so I don't want you to work too hard."

"Thank you. I will do my best. I will have to get another job when I'm out of school though, because I will need steady work."

"Yes, yes, I know you will, Elsie. You will need a full time job."

"Mama, I have been offered a job in Coleraine. I will stay with Ruthie and go to work from there," Elsie told her mama.

"I hate to see you go Elsie. I know I will miss you terribly. It will seem different without you around."

"I know, and I will miss you so much, Mama, but we need more money, so I can help you and Daddy a little bit to pay our bills."

After being there a few days, Elsie was happy with her newfound freedom.

"I will be living in Coleraine now, Viola. After I leave, you will have to take over. Hope you can manage our home when I'm gone."

"I will be OK. I'll do the same things you did," Viola answered.

Going to school and caring for the younger ones was a little hectic, while also doing their job to keep the family together. It was expected for each child to take over the household when their turn came. It was a necessity, and each one understood this without reservation.

"How would you like to work for me?" The little ten-year-old girl was startled at the sound of the voice so close behind her. Without hesitation, she answered, "Yes, I will help you," when she recognized the lady who was talking.

"You can help with the ironing, dishes, clip the grass along the sidewalk, and other jobs. I will give you fifty cents a week."

She was not paid one penny for working the whole summer. Perhaps giving her dinner and supper daily was her pay. She had been taught to help others, therefore the money did not enter her mind. She didn't tell her parents she had not been paid. It simply did not matter that much. The Great Depression was hard on everyone, so perhaps this lady could not pay the fifty cents a week, which was promised this girl.

Chapter 21

Often these children worked for different people with the same results. They never saw the money they earned. When one family needed help to move to another town, they asked one of the girls to go along to care for their children. She thought when they were settled, they would take her home, but they never mentioned it. Day after day passed; and she wanted to be with her family. With no way to contact her daddy, she stayed longer and longer. Homesick and lonely, she put her belongings in a bag, went to the corner where two roads met and hoped someone would stop and take her home. She didn't know how far it was. She only knew how badly she wanted to be home.

I don't think these nice people had any money to buy gasoline is why they didn't take me home, she thought, as she stood waiting for someone—anyone—to give her a ride back to Harrisville, where she lived. After she stood in the hot sun for some time, a car finally stopped to give her a ride.

~≫ The Love of Annie

"What in the world are you doing, here? Why are you standing on this corner in this hot sun? You must be roasting," the lady said to the young girl.

"I didn't know how I could get home, and I want to go home," was her answer.

"Wouldn't the people you babysat for take you home?"

"Yes, they said they would some day," was her answer.

"Well, get in the car. We are going to Harrisville, and we will take you home."

"Thank you. Why did you stop? Did you recognize me?"

"Well, honey," they said, "the hot sun was beating down on you, and when we stopped, we recognized you. Anyway, we could not pass anyone up standing in that sun without offering a ride. It is really hot, but we will be home soon."

When they got home, Annie's and Howard's daughter thanked them. "I am so glad to be home. Thank you!"

"We are glad it was us who came by."

"Thanks again," she said as she got out of the car.

"Oh, honey, one more thing. Did you think to get the money you earned before you left?"

"Money? No, no, I didn't think of it. I just wanted to be home, and I'm sure they didn't have any money to pay me."

During this time, Annie didn't seem to get any better. Life was stressful. She was a lovely person, such a beautiful person, yet no one could help her. She had once shown so much love for her Howard, but this was changing. Now, all to soon, you would never have known that she cared for him at all.

Every move Howard made seemed to go against her. Everything he said sent her into a frenzy. She would not talk to Howard—only a word or two, once in awhile.

The Love of Annie

One day, thinking Annie was in her room, Howard went into the kitchen (Annie was doing things so out of the ordinary these days). He didn't see her in the kitchen until it was too late. This day she became very angry when she saw Howard. She picked up a glass and was about to throw it across the room where Howard and two of the children were standing. Howard was afraid one of them would get injured, so he quickly stepped in front of the children to protect them.

"Mom," he said, "I have never raised a hand to you in my life. But if you throw that glass, I will have to protect the children."

Not having heard their daddy say or do anything that sounded even remotely harsh, the two frightened children ran out the door and hid under the big porch. They were too young to know this had to be said to prevent things from getting worse. The quick movement of the children running, got Annie's attention and she put the glass slowly back on the table. Howard quickly went to check on the girls. Finding they were OK, he explained the situation, and then went on his way to get at his work.

Annie had always loved company, especially Howard's family. They loved her very much also.

"Annie, you are such a happy person," Howard's sister once remarked. "We enjoy coming here, but I think we come too often."

"Nonsense," was Annie's reply. "We have so much fun playing dominoes. I wish you could come more often. Sometime maybe we will be lucky enough to beat our men one game. Amy, we love it when you come. We truly like having you. I thought you knew that," Annie told her as they were preparing to leave.

"Yes, Annie, we do. But we are here so much more than you come to our house."

"Well, Amy, it's easier for us to be close to the children, and we love having you, so don't worry about coming here too often."

This attitude came to an end quite abruptly. Annie turned away from relatives. She treated them coolly, not meeting them at the door when they came and not bidding them goodbye when they left. And she would no longer play dominoes with them. It was obvious she was glad they were going home. Not understanding the reason for this change in Annie's attitude and treatment, they came less often, then not at all. Howard could not understand how his Annie could treat his family so badly. Even less, he understood how her love for him had turned to such hate.

Annie sat for long periods of time and didn't seem to be aware of her surroundings. When Howard wanted to talk to Annie, she would tell him to get out. "Get out! "Get out of here! Get out of this room!" she would scream. Hurt and bewildered, Howard would meekly back out of her room, pleading with Annie to let him talk to her.

Time after time, Howard would go to her room. "Mom, . . . Mom, . . . Please let me come in. Mom, I love you. I love you so much! Please, can I come in? I only want to talk to you." But he was always met with anger and hostility.

"Get out of here! Don't you ever set foot in here again! Do you hear me? Get out! Get out!"

"All right. All right, Mom. I'll go. But why? Why, Mom? We have always loved each other so much and . . . Mom, . . . I still care so much for you. I want so badly to make things right for you."

"Get out!" she screamed.

Howard tried to stay out of her sight so as not to upset her. He worked every free minute he had. Week after week went by without a word from his Annie. After so much time had passed, the yearning to see her, to touch her, to just hold her again, proved too much for him. The only time he saw Annie at all was if one of the children went into the room, which Howard and Annie no longer shared. He would sometimes get a glimpse of her as the door opened or closed. Howard felt such an overwhelming need to talk to her.

One day his need was so strong, he prepared a meal himself and took it to her room, hoping she would be glad or at least show some sign of caring for him. And maybe, just maybe, it would bring back the beautiful memories of the years ago when he cooked dinner every Sunday. Remembering the happiness and love they once shared, for a minute he really believed Annie would still love him. He hoped she would at least care enough to remember the happiness they once had, if only for a moment.

Annie had a cup of coffee sitting on top of the old stove. When Howard knocked, then gently opened the door to her room, Annie jumped to her feet, grabbed the coffee cup, and threw it at Howard. As he leaned to pick it up, she slammed the door. He had never seen his Annie like this before, and it troubled him greatly.

At last he decided to talk to the country doctor again. Dr. McCleaster had known Annie for many years, and this behavior was not Annie, the quiet-spoken, beautiful lady of the past. He gave Howard some different medicine "This should help her. See that she takes this every day. I'll be back in a week or so to check on her."

The new drug did help. Annie became calmer, but she would not let Howard give her the medicine, so the children gave it to her. Not a big change could be seen, but enough to keep her home with her family. Though she didn't do much work, she could be home and was more like herself, until the news came that her mother had died.

By the time Annie had married and settled down, she was very close to her mother, so this was another setback. At first she seemed to handle her loss quite well. But after a while, she paced the floor or sat again for longer periods of time with a cup of coffee sitting on top of the stove. Annie always had a cup of coffee sitting on the stove.

Ethel and Gladys were playing near by and overheard their mama say, "She's not dead yet! She's not dead!" These strange words being said by their mama frightened them. They ran from the house to get their sisters.

"You kids know how much we love our mama. We don't want her to die, so she didn't want her mama to die either," Elsie explained.

As time went on, the family often heard Annie talking when there was no one there to answer her.

Chapter 22

"It is really dark out there!" exclaimed Howard "Those clouds are really black, and I'm sure there is wind in them. We sure seem to be getting a lot of storms here lately. Looks like we are going to get some rain anyway." As Howard went about his evening chores, milking the cow he called Whitey, and slopping his pigs, the wind began to blow.

The little ones scampered close to Mama. "The wind won't upset our house, Mama, will it? Will the wind upset our house? I'm scared, Mama," cried the younger ones.

As Annie watched the wind get stronger and stronger, she leaned over and put her still loving arms around them.

"No, no, pets. I'm here. Our home is not a high house. It is a low one, so the wind will blow over the top of it. We will be safe.

"Are you afraid, Mama?"

"No, pet, I'm not afraid. The storm will pass by, and you will see, we'll be fine." Her comforting way and her

The Love of Annie

reassuring words eased their fears. As usual, the storm did pass over, and the little ones went about their playing again.

By now Annie had turned her formerly undying love for Howard into a bitterness and a hate beyond repair. Howard finally realized the sight of him made her more upset, so he desperately tried to stay out of her way and out of her sight completely.

This was something the children could not comprehend. They had known nothing but love and kindness between their parents all the years before. Now that was gone, and they witnessed mostly silence or an extreme anger toward their daddy.

With Annie being ill, living in the same house was not easy for Howard. Annie came out of her room only to grab a bite to eat or to wash out her white aprons. What few she had left were badly worn, but she still loved wearing them.

Howard learned to time himself. He made sure he had something to do outside, so as not to upset his Annie. Knowing she liked her white aprons to stay white, he made sure he did not cause any disturbance by coming into the house while she was washing them. He did odd jobs until she was through.

Annie was still a very pretty lady. She wore a white apron every day and pinned a pink ribbon in her hair.

Howard tried with every ounce of energy he had to keep his family together, though the county nurse often talked to him about putting the children in an orphanage.

"You love them and want what is best for them, I know," the nurse said. "Mr. DeVault, it's obvious that you cannot support them. In an orphanage, they will be fed and well taken care of."

"Yes," Howard retorted, "that they may be. I'm sure they would be fed, but, no, no, no, not ever will I give up my children! Not ever, ever, ever, will I give up my children! Do you hear me? No one! No one can ever take my children from me!"

The nurse turned and walked out the door. "I will be back again. You absolutely cannot keep the children. I will be back." True to her word, a few days later, she was at Howard's door again. This time a tall gentleman was with her.

"Howard, I'm from the orphanage in Cadiz. How are you today, Mr. DeVault?"

"Well, to tell you the truth I am fine. But if you are here to take my children, I'm afraid you had better leave right now."

"Well, I really came to explain to you how well the children would be treated at the orphanage. Please, may I come in?"

"Yes. Come in," Howard told him.

"The children will be well-fed and clothed. They will each be expected to have some work to do, and that's it," the gentleman explained.

"Well, I'm sure you will understand when I say they need their parents love. And sir, this is something you can't give to my kids."

"With so many people working there, they will have lots of love and care," the man replied.

"Sir, I just told you they need our love, and our love is what they are going to get. As I said before, my children are staying right here. I know I can't feed them as well as you can, but we have made it this long. Things have to get better; no way can it get any worse. Now once and for all, you are not going to take my children. Do you understand? They are mine! Mine! Do you hear me? Only over my dead body will you take them. Now please go. I love my family, and they are not going to be put in an orphanage."

Howard was so relieved when the county nurse and the gentleman left. Feeling he had settled it once and for all, he tried to put it out of his mind. Every so often the matter to get a better home for the children was brought up again, but Howard held fast to his decision. No one was ever going to take his children from him.

Howard was still working for the WPA and the coal mine when they had a little work and were not striking. He could never get ahead, however, no matter how hard he tried. There were too many odds against him.

Howard felt the crunch more and more, because he had to watch over Annie more than usual. In the past, it had been Annie who was there by Howard's side to encourage him and help keep his spirits high. Now Howard had to be there to watch over his Annie. Together, they tried to keep their hopes high for a better tomorrow, especially during the few times Annie felt like her old self, the way she had been before the economy got so bad and before the Great Depression had swept the country.

When Mr. Williams, the bill collector, came to the door one day to collect some money Howard owed him, Mr. Williams raised his voice, and it frightened the little ones. He was very angry. "Mr. DeVault," he said, "I want my money! Now if I don't get it, I will have to take more drastic measures to get my money." His voice was loud and firm, and it scared the little ones. They thought this strange man was going to take their daddy away from them.

As the man was threatening Howard, one of the youngsters held tight to his daddy's leg.

The Love of Annie

"Please don't take my daddy! Please don't take him away! I love him."

When Mr. Williams realized the child's fear of losing his daddy, he relented a little and then left.

"Daddy, he can't take you away from us, can he, Daddy? He ain't going to come back again, is he?"

"No," Howard said, "He won't come back. Don't worry, I have a bit that will help. Now run along and play, OK?" Howard flinched, knowing he had no money, but he had to calm the little one's fears.

WPA gave work to help the needy. It was hard work, grubbing out trees, working on the road, digging ditches, and so on. Howard needed the work so badly; he would go at a moment's notice, so they would have something to put on the table to eat.

The town kids would tease the workers at times to try to cheer them up a little. "WPA, we poke along," they would holler to the men working as they walked by. "Isn't that what WPA means? We poke along?" They all knew better by the way the men were perspiring. They only wanted to add a little fun to another extra hard day in the hot sun the men had to endure.

The WPA was a job for the very needy—a worker's pay assistance, of sort. Of course, the kids were told to come and help them. "We will see that the work is plentiful, enough today to go around, and you kids can work, and we will poke around," the men would yell back to the kids.

The kids would just laugh. "No, that's all right. You're doing such a good job, we don't want to ruin a good thing," they'd holler as they went on their way.

Working for the WPA and the coal mine when he had a day's work, along with his other jobs that needed attended to, kept Howard busy. He didn't have time to worry, but his prayers were always for the safety of all families.

Often, when a coal mine had a cave-in, many other miners rushed to see if they could be of help. Now and then there would be a cave-in, and the miners would be trapped in the back of a mine for hours and hours. And many times they never made it out alive.

One particular cave-in happened on a hot summer day. Several coal miners were trapped inside. Each miner tried desperately to keep the others awake and not let anyone go to sleep. If they went to sleep, the gas fumes would kill them very quickly. One of the coal miners kept a little diary every day of his life in the mines. His diary was a small pad he took along with him to the coal mines. Other miners often did the same. They never knew if they would get out alive.

Each day these men were trapped in this dungeon called a workplace, this man wrote exactly how each of his fellow miners and friends were holding up. As the first miner began to show weakness, he wrote "Bill (or whatever the miner's name happened to be), is going to be leaving us soon. His head is beginning to drop a little. He is so weak; it won't be long now. Oh my, Oh, . . . oh, . . . he is gone. Well, . . . he is gone. Our buddy could hold on to his precious life no longer; he just died at 12:30 this twelfth day of July (or whatever day it happened to be)." He made sure to put the exact date, time, and month, so their loved ones could at least know when his suffering and fears had all ended. He also wrote the last words each coal miner said before he died.

When the next miner began to show signs of losing ground and weakness, he, like all of the others, would at times be incoherent and mixed up. "Right now he seemingly is rational again. He wanted to live so badly, as we all do. Now, all too quickly, he is dead. I thought for a minute he would make a comeback, but he, too, is gone. The last words he said just before he died were, 'If I go first, and any of you are left to get out of this hole alive, please tell my wife and children I loved them to the end. Please tell them, will you? Please . . . please . . . tell them how badly I wanted to get back home to them.' His head began to lean forward as he whispered his final words. 'Please . . . tell . . . them . . . I loved . . . them. . . . Good . . . bye.'

"Now there are not many of us left," he wrote. "We talk often about which of us will be the next in line to die. Our spirits are good, considering the ordeal we are going through. One of us tries to tell a joke to keep up the morale of the others. The men and I pray all of the time. We know that our chance of survival is not good at all."

He kept writing in his book about each miner the best way he knew how. To save on light, they used only one carbide light at a time. When it began to get dim, they used another one, then another. The miner writing this diary wrote that some of the men became delirious a few hours before they died. When he got to the last miner other than himself, he wrote. "My last buddy is delirious now. It hurts so much to know that when he is gone, I will be the only one left. He is talking out of his head. I can hardly hear him now; his words are jumbled. He is saying things that I can't make out; he is delirious. I know he won't be with me much longer. Oh, . . . oh, . . . I'm afraid he is gone. He is lying so still. Yes, his head just dropped. He is gone. I'm alone. Now I'm all alone. My last buddy and friend just died."

He kept his diary up to the moment he himself could hold on to his precious life no longer. The words barely legible, "I'm the only one left now. It doesn't look like I will make it." His words trailed off of the paper. Again, trying with all the strength and effort he could muster, he scribbled, "How I love you. Goodbye . . . good . . . good . . . bye. . . ."

These were his last words. When, at long last, the rescue squad arrived, his pencil and diary (the words scrawled unevenly) lay by his slumped body. The carbide lights had burned out, as had their lives. This was one of the things all miners had to face at the mines with fear daily. Yet the Great Depression had taken such a toll on so many families, the men were happy to go to work, no matter how much danger was involved.

When Howard returned home after walking three miles from the mines and after picking coal all day, sometimes he was so tired he would feel like going to a chair and staying for the night. One thing that kept him from doing it was his children. Though he was tired and bent, he would never let on. He knew one of his children would inevitably grab their daddy around his waist, put their feet on each of his feet as he carried them into the kitchen and across the floor, never once complaining of being tired or the children being too heavy. He was just happy to have work and glad to be home to hear the words, "Daddy, give me a ride on your foot." He had the strength and stamina because of the love he had for his family. They meant more to him than being tired.

This was more than most people would do, especially on the days he had only hard biscuits and a little lard to eat for his dinner. Biscuits were made with little or no shortening. Lard was spread on top of the biscuit to add a wee bit of flavor. This was not much to eat when digging and picking coal all day.

"Sparky," one of the town boys said, "you work so hard to get those kids big. Why don't you knock them in the head and raise pigs?"

"Well, Bucky," he said, "you are right, it probably would be cheaper. But it's funny, I can't pick which one to start with, so I might as well keep them all."

"Yeah, I knew you figured that way. You can't say I didn't try to help."

"You are right again," said Sparky.

"Look at you tired, and worn out. Your kids want a free ride, and on your feet, yet," Bucky quipped.

"You're right again, but the way I see it, that's the only thing that's free, so let them do it while they can. And I love it when they run to meet me and grab my lunch bucket. They know that I always save a bite or two for them. What little there is to save makes me happy."

"Oh Sparky, you're just too soft, and you'll never change. And since I can't get a rise out of you, I'll see you later, Sparky."

"All right, Bucky, I'll see you. And, by the way, Bucky, if and when you can ever come up with something better than that, I might even give it a thought. Until you get another brainstorm like that one, guess I'll just keep plugging along as I have always done."

Knock the kids in the head and raise pigs. . . . I wonder where that boy gets those funny ideas? He seems to lay awake at night dreaming all that up. Quite a Bucky, he thought as he went back to his work.

Bucky was one of his favorite teenagers that met daily at Howard and Annie's home.

As the town kids grew to be young men and women several of the young girls married one of the boys who had

~≽ The Love of Annie

met at this home. Howard was so pleased when this happened. Howard often said, "I bet Hallie and Don will end up getting married before too long. Yes, I'm sure they will. And I'll bet a dollar to a doughnut, Halford and Betty will get married." He felt pretty smug whenever one couple did marry, and he was most always right in his predictions. Howard loved these kids so much.

While Howard was thinking about the town kids, the bad news came that Johnny had been injured in the coal mine. This time it was not life threatening, but it was bad enough—a back injury. "Always something, always something," Howard remarked.

After being laid up for some time, Johnny again went back to work, only to get his hand caught somehow between a vein of coal and the machine he worked on, called "the joy." This time he had his hand mashed and two of his fingers cut off. Troubles hovered over this family like none other. There was no end for Annie and Howard.

But with the love of God and the hope of a better tomorrow, they got through each day. "One day at a time" as Annie had always told her beloved Howard.

Because Johnny was married and on his own, it was not a hardship on them financially, but it added more stress for Annie. It was a sad thing to cope with when any miner was injured in the mines, but when it was your own son, the worry was much greater.

Chapter 23

One afternoon Annie was alone in her room, while Howard and the children finished their dinner. The dishes were still on the table when it began to get dark very suddenly. The sky looked ominous—very dark, and oh, so still. There was not one trace of a breeze, not a leaf moving—so still, so very still. It felt as though the whole town was sleeping. No one could be seen anywhere. Odd shades of light strewn amongst the ghastly, dark black clouds gave an eerie feeling.

Everyone felt as if there was no one left in the town except themselves. It was such a traumatic, frightening feeling as they stood watching, waiting, . . . waiting, . . . waiting for the unknown to happen. Feeling alone amidst the massive, hideous-looking sky gave everyone a fear unheard of before.

As Howard and his family stood so still, almost as though they were paralyzed, the darkness surrounded them. It seemed like night instead of mid-day. Finally, Howard began to move around to try to lessen the fear the children were experiencing. He went from one door to the other, then to the windows to check what was happening. Terror filled all their hearts.

When they heard a voice outside, they went to the door to find out who was talking. An airplane was flying over very low, advertising Casey's Oil. The advertisement was very loud and clear. But not a whisper of wind. So still, so, so, very still. Everyone had this eerie feeling that something devastating was about to take place. The ghastly, moving clouds and the darkness were extremely terrifying, filling people with terror for what seemed an eternity. But, in actuality, it was only an hour or so. The man in the airplane was advertising oil when suddenly he was gone. Being in a small plane, one could only hope that he survived. The fear surrounding the people was almost more than one could cope with.

Everyone stood quietly, watching with such anticipation of what was taking place. Never had anyone seen a sky so ominous, so frightening. Even the small children hovered close to their parents in fear. The darkness enveloped the whole town. The air was so heavy; it was hard to breathe. As Howard, Viola, Ethel, and Gladys stood in the kitchen looking out the door and seeing the airplane disappear amongst the hideous black clouds, Viola said, "Daddy, we had better close this door. A storm will come and take our house."

Annie's door was ajar, and Howard looked in to see how she was holding up. With such a frightening experience going on, he was concerned about her. It was evident that he feared for her and the family. He turned very quickly when he heard Viola's words about the house being taken.

Just moments before, the unheard-of calm, never before felt in this small community, was terrifying. In the calm, the silence was felt so vividly, one could feel his skin crawling from sheer fear. The air was so heavy. Then suddenly, a terrible noise seemed to come from the sky. It was a hissing sound, then a roaring sort of a noise. One would think it was the rumble of a train passing close by. The fast-moving black clouds were rolling and tumbling so fast, and in the blink of an eye, a huge black cloud began to roll into circles as it made its way to the ground in what seemed to be a slanting line.

The circling motion of the clouds descended from the sky with such a display of force, it sent those who were watching to shelter quickly. In a fraction of time, the tornado funnel hit in a field just below Howard and Annie's home. The ground was a mass of dust going in a wild circling motion. What had been moments before a calm so frightening, had now turned into a devastating array of turmoil and confusion, so that Howard did not know what to do. The tornado hit so quickly, the calm turned into a roaring, hideous noise. Everything was sheer turmoil. The fear he had for his family, and especially for his Annie, was too much for Howard to contend with alone.

Very quickly, the wind became very fierce, picking up momentum by the second. One hinge fell off of the door, and it took all the strength the children and Howard had to push the kitchen table against the door to keep it in place. The wind became stronger and stronger. Nothing could hold back the inferno rage of this wind. As the door flew open, the noise was loud and hideous. Pots, pans, clothing, just everything went flying around! Suddenly the roof was gone from the newer part of the house. The walls began to waver. Things were happening so fast one could hardly think. Howard yelled, "Run to Milt's! Run to Milt's!" Milt's was

~≼ The Love of Annie

the barbershop directly across the road from Howard and Annie's home and the closest place for the children to run for safety.

"Hold tight to each other. Run! Run! Come on, Mom, we have to get out of here!" Mom would not go. "Mom!" he hollered, "we have to get out of here, or we are going to die. Come on, Mom! Come on!"

"No, no, I'm not going," Annie said.

"Go! Go!" he hollered to the kids. "Hurry! Run straight across the road. I'll stay with Mom. Run! Run!" Viola carried Dixie, Ethel carried Anna Lee while holding on to Gladys's and Billy's hands, they ran straight across the road to the town's barbershop.

Milt was watching this awful storm also when he saw the children coming. After opening his door to let the children in, it seemed utterly impossible to close it again. Everyone pushed with every ounce of strength they had. Finally, exhausted, they got the door closed and locked, but not before the barbershop was riddled with Milt's own belongings. "What a fiendish storm! What an awful storm!" Milt kept repeating.

As they sat frantic and helpless, listening and watching, some of the boards from Howard and Annie's house plunged into Milt's house. What a terrifying thing! Little Billy cried out, "Save me, Milt! Save me, Milt! I'm scared! Save me!" Milt was as scared as any of them, but he reached down and touched little Billy on his arm.

"I'm trying, Billy. I'm trying, but I have all I can do to save myself."

It was so frightening. It sounded as though Milt's house, too, was breaking into bits and pieces. The hellish sound of debris hitting against the house and windows was terrifying. There seemed to be no escape.

Though Milt's house had a cellar, there was no access to it from the inside of his home. To try to get to the outside cellar door would have been utterly impossible. It would be certain death for someone, or perhaps all of them. The cellar door was on the wrong side of the house, in the exact path of the tornado. Milt dispelled any thought of trying to make it to the cellar.

Trying to comfort Howard and Annie's children while he himself didn't know what to do was not easy. He was not sure if his own home could stand up under this horrendous wind. He kept trying to ease the fear of the children and himself. He repeated over and over again, "It is almost over. It will stop pretty soon. The wind will stop pretty soon." Saying it would stop soon did not mean that it would, but he was trying with all of his being to comfort the kids' fears. The inferno strength of the wind kept right on blowing. Each minute it picked up momentum. Panic was on everyone's face.

When the boards from the house across the road—the boards from the children's home—landed on Milt's roof, he thought that his home would also be blown away. The little ones stared at Milt, but their begging him to help them only made him feel more helpless. Knowing he was unable to do anything but wait out the storm frightened him even more.

His fear and anxiety were so intense that he paced the floor, glancing quickly out of the window, not wanting the little ones to see how scared he really was. He'd pace the floor back and forth, back and forth, stopping only a second to try to reassure the children. Then he would walk some more. Suddenly the wind seemed to stop blowing. After such a fiendish wind, it seemed impossible that it would stop so suddenly. Milt went to the window. "I think it's over, I think the storm is all over."

He opened the door and looked out to make sure it was safe again. He gasped, "Oh my! Oh my! Your house is gone! Oh my! Your house is gone! Oh . . . it's gone! Looks like there is one room standing. Yes, yes, there is one room left. Only one room out of the whole house is left. We had better see if your mama and daddy are all right."

As the children hurried out the door, Viola said, "Mama's room is still there. Just Mama's room is left! I hope Mama and Daddy are all right. Let's go home and see if they are OK." They hurried to get home to see if their parents were safe. As they went across the road nothing was the same. What they saw did not seem real. It was more like a bad dream. Their home was gone.

The children burst in through the door that was already half-opened because of the tornado. Howard and Annie were numb from the agony and fear of what had just happened—numb, not only for the children's safety, but also for their own safety. The children were so happy when they saw their parents were safe. Annie and Howard quickly embraced them. It was hard to believe the miracle, that through such a tornado no one had been injured or killed.

What was once Howard and Annie's home was gone. The tornado had ripped the house apart like kindling wood. The roof and walls had started ripping apart while the children were yet in the home.

The older ones got the younger children out in time to find refuge at the town barbershop and not any too soon. There was nothing left except one room—the room that

The Love of Annie

Annie had claimed for her own for some time. It was the room that Howard was forbidden to ever step his foot into—the room in which poor, sick Annie could find only a fraction of peace, if any.

This was the finishing touch for Annie. The once beautiful lady could no longer be a helper and a lover to Howard. Now, even more than before, she turned her abounding love into an inferno of hate toward him. Not understanding it all, broke Howard's heart. Yet, patient, loving Howard still lived with the hope that Annie would someday realize her illness and love him again.

Chapter 24

The tornado was finally over, but not before leaving a devastating path of destruction behind. Furniture, clothing, boards, and debris of all kinds was scattered around. Nothing was left but the bare floors of this modest home. The family's belongings were strewn all over this small town.

The door to Annie's room had to be fixed temporarily until more help arrived. The children looked on in disbelief that their beds were no longer there. Not knowing this terrible thing would soon separate them, they climbed up on the floor, which only a few minutes before had been their bedroom, and now saw everything was gone. They didn't realize or understand they had no place to sleep any more. Their lives would never be the same. Not ever again. Not ever again could their lives be the same.

As the cameramen from the newspapers took pictures to cover this terrible tragedy and asked questions about why Annie would not leave her room, they realized Annie's illness. So they took pictures of the damage and went on about their work.

This tornado was the last thing Annie needed. It completely broke her. Annie could no longer reason with life at all. This had been the last straw. The threads she had left to hold on to had long ago worn thin and were now, oh, so fragile. She completely escaped into her own little world.

Annie was so ill that Howard would not leave her side. He knew help would be coming, so he tried to comfort Annie as much as he could, but it was to no avail. By now, she was more bitter toward Howard and a lot more so toward the rest of his family, especially his brothers and sisters. Her personality had completely changed. She was a different person. She was no longer the sweet, loving person she use to be, welcoming everyone with open arms. That was the Annie of days gone by. Now she wanted only to be alone in her own little world. She had lost touch with reality.

For several days after the storm, people came to see the terrible damage this horrendous storm had left in its path. Ruthie and Johnny came home to help as much as possible. They made temporary plans for shelter. The neighbors were so kind to offer a bed for the children that night. Thinking Bobby was at a friend's house, they began to worry something had happened to him when he didn't come home after the tornado had passed. With so much happening, another fear took over, Bobby was gone. Where was Bobby? Panic set in. Everyone was crying and wondering where is little brother Bobby? Although the tornado had passed, with so much commotion, they had not realized Bobby had not come home.

They were frightened. Being in such a hurry to save the lives of those in the house, no one had time to think who was present or who wasn't. Their only thought was to find safety. Now Bobby presented more worry. They had to find him. The fear that he was lost in the storm was traumatic. Fear kept mounting as they decided the best way to start looking for him. The mind-boggling experience of such a disaster was almost too much to comprehend. The one thing now was to find Bobby and then plan where to go with the family.

The sky again began to get very dark, and the same eerie feeling set in. People commented that they thought another tornado would hit soon. They had to be prepared in case it did happen.

Bobby had to be found. With another storm seemingly brewing, he would not have a chance if he were out there without protection.

"Oh how scared he must be. But where is he?" they kept asking themselves. "Maybe he is hurt or something even worse," one of them commented.

While trying to cope with the situation and not knowing where to start, they heard someone coming. Bobby came up from behind them and asked, "Dad, do you know where I was at when the storm hit so hard?"

"Oh, oh Bobby, you are safe! Are you all right? You are OK! Thank God. We were getting awfully scared, trying to decide how to find you. Where were you, Bobby? For goodness sakes, where were you?"

Everyone talked at once asking his whereabouts. Bobby, a bit shaken and tired, said that when the storm hit, he was in the woods. He loved the woods as much as Howard and Annie did. But all alone out there, the wind so strong and the trees falling so closely beside him, was frightening.

"Dad," he said, "there were trees falling everywhere around me. They had me closed in. The limbs and branches were hitting me, but they didn't hurt too much. I could see the branches and limbs flying past me, so I found a great big tree and I leaned against it. I held on to it so tight, Dad, but I was afraid the tree would fall on me. I was sure scared, so I held on tighter. I kept thinking, I can't hold on much longer. My hands hurt so bad. I was afraid I was going to get blown away. I kept saying, 'please help me to hold on. Please, God! Help me to hold on.' I thought I wouldn't be able to hold tight until the tornado had passed. Being alone in the woods was scary, Dad."

"I know, son, I know. It must have been quite a thing to go through. Now you are safe, and we're happy that you are home. You can't know how frightening it was. You out there and maybe hurt or pinned under a tree with no one knowing where you were or how to find you in such a storm as this. At first we thought you were at one of your friends, but when you didn't come home right after the storm, we were so afraid you were injured or something else had happened to you."

Howard was grateful his family all survived such an ordeal. "So much has happened, and now that Bobby is safe through all this, we have to thank God. A six-room house, Mom so sick, and her room the only room left out of six, has to be a miracle. God was still watching over us. For some reason he saved Mom's room, and no one was hurt. He knew Mom's condition, and he protected us all. I don't want any one of you to forget this day. God did take care of us!"

"Don't worry, Dad, I won't forget it! I won't ever forget it," Bobby replied. He was still shaken from the fear of being blown away and maybe no one finding him.

Johnny decided he could take Ethel and Dixie to live with them. Ruthie took Gladys, Billy, Anna Lee, and Mama to live with her. "Since we are living with Grandpa, he will be glad to have Mama at home with him again. He was so close to Mama when she was young," Ruthie said.

"Viola, would you stay with us? You can help with the children and housework," the next-door neighbor asked.

"Yes, I'll stay with you and help with your work," she answered.

Bobby and Howard were going to "batch" in the one forlorn room that was left. Howard decided Bobby would be good company for him. Besides, Bobby loved his daddy so much, he would be sad if he couldn't be with him. Howard found himself thinking how Bobby had become a man overnight. Suddenly he seemed older.

The children all had a place to live until a permanent home could be found. Life was not the same, however. This loving family had to split up in different directions. It was quite a heart-breaking experience for a family with so much love for each other. Time passed so slowly. Being separated was a different way of life and hard for the younger ones to grasp.

In the meantime, an uncle asked if Gladys could live with them during the summer months. He said, "It would be company for my youngest daughter. They would get along well, and it would be one less for you to take care of, Ruth. You have to take care of yourself, too, you know."

"Well, if she wants to go until things get straightened out, that would be fine. Then we'll see what happens," Ruthie answered. "But this has to be her decision."

Gladys packed up her things and went to live with her uncle and aunt until other arrangements could be made. She had been there only a few days when she wanted to see her mama again. Her aunt told the girls they could walk up

The Love of Annie

the pike to see her. The next day, they decided that since it was such a nice day, it would be a perfect time for a walk. The two started on the trek to see her mother and the others who were staying there, also.

She missed her mama. She and the other children combed her hair or rubbed her forehead when she didn't feel well. With no fans, or any way to keep cool, the heat was too much for Annie. At times, she would ask if one of the children would please take a newspaper, fold it, and fan her for only a few minutes. Since they did not own a fan, they were happy to do this to make her feel better.

Having a bad heart made Annie's condition worse. Each of the children loved her so dearly, they would do as she asked without hesitation.

The girls enjoyed walking up the Martins Ferry Pike and decided they would go there again later. For now, it satisfied them to see the rest of the family was all right and close enough they could go again.

All signs of Annie's illness pointed to the dire need for more help than she could get at home. Annie couldn't sleep at night and walked the floors all night long. Ruthie knew Annie's behavior was not normal. She kept a close watch over her mama, not feeling secure in her behavior.

Annie was so protective of her father. She loved him very much. He had kept her going those years when she was still living at home with her parents, and her life seemed to be in such turmoil. She and her father were still very close. Annie's father was happy when Ruthie brought her to live with them temporarily, until other arrangements could be made.

Suddenly, there was a noticeable change in Annie. The way she watched her father changed. It was a total change in her behavior, at least where he was concerned. Ruthie checked on Grandpa (Annie's father) regularly. This was Grandpa's home, and Ruthie and her family lived there to take care of him. She knew his needs and provided them for him. She saw the change in Annie's attitude and felt her grandfather, being in a wheelchair, definitely needed to be watched.

When Ruthie found Grandpa lying on the floor one day, she became frightened. "Grandpa, what happened? What happened?" Not wanting to hurt Ruthie's feelings, he just waved his hand. "Help me to get up, Ruthie. I'm fine. Just help me to get up."

"Are you all right, Grandpa? Did you get hurt when you fell?"

"No, no! I'm OK. I am not hurt."

Annie had apparently tried to get him out of his wheelchair, and he had fallen. Grandpa was not able to get up by himself. When Ruthie found Annie standing over her father, it frightened her.

The family knew something had to be done to protect others and to protect Annie. After talking to Dr. McCleaster, the decision was made to get help for Annie. Sadly, they had to commit her to the mental hospital.

Not knowing their mama had been taken to the hospital, Gladys and Vivian went again to see her. On the way, they stopped to see her aunt for a few minutes. Since she lived only two houses from where Annie was staying, they decided to visit her before going on.

"Well," her aunt Elda said firmly, "you have to know, so I might just as well tell you. You will find out anyway. They took your mother away today."

"Who took Mama away? Where did they take Mama?" Gladys asked.

"They took her to a hospital, but you can't go see her. It is too far."

Not wanting to hear this, and not really grasping what she meant, the girls hurried out the door and went on their way.

Ruthie quickly put her arms around them and explained how sick Mama was. "Honey, I know the doctors will help her. Please, don't cry. Please don't cry. I feel bad when I see you crying. She had to go away so she can get well again and come back to us. Then she can come home and be with us maybe real soon," she told the two girls.

With so many changes in such a short period of time, the children did not understand why everything was so different for them. One change after another added more hurt and more fear of the unknown for the children. They tried to hide their feelings, but the hurt they felt was plain to see.

The Depression and losing her homes, especially the home she had loved so much on the hill, was hard for Annie to put out of her mind completely. There had been too many hardships and too much suffering. There was never enough money to pay bills. With such a large family to feed, it was more than she could take, especially when wondering each day where they could rake up enough food to feed them. The tornado was so destructive, leaving them with out a place to lay their heads. This took its toll on poor Annie. It changed her whole being. With so much grief to always endure, she lost herself completely. It was enough to test the mettle of anyone. With the hope of getting help for her, she was put in a mental ward in a state hospital.

Summer was coming to an end, and still there was no solution to what the future would hold. Howard's brothers saw the dilemma he was in and built a home for his family.

Work started on it immediately. In the meantime, the children went to school, but some of them in other towns, since they were living in different homes. This was not a happy time for this family.

Mr. and Mrs. Ed Kliner were good people and realizing the trauma the family was in, asked if Gladys could live with them. They said they would send her to school so she could attend the same one she had gone to before. She was happy to be there because she was only a block or so from her old home and her daddy. She went to one place, then to another, and finally to Kliners, so she could start school when it was time.

The Kliners were very good to her and treated her as if she were their own child.

The new house was completed quite fast. Elsie decided to come home again to help her daddy. By now, he was critically ill with a goiter. He had one goiter, and for some reason, a second goiter grew quite soon after the first surgery. He was very ill, and the doctor called the family to the hospital. He was sure Howard would not live. But with his daughter's help nursing him back to health, he recovered sooner then was expected.

Howard had been lonely with all his family in different places, and he was happy when Elsie came back to get the new home ready. They worked long hours so the children could be home again.

On Christmas Eve, Elsie and Howard brought the children back home, so they could be together. It was so good to have the family in one place, especially on Christmas Eve, so they could feel the magic of Christmas as much as possible.

Everyone was happy to be home, but nothing was the same. Something else was different—it was the new home.

It was really nice, but the old memories were not the same. It was so unlike the warm, loving feeling the old home had represented.

Howard became quiet. "How I wish Mom could be here, Oh, how I have missed her," he said. For a moment, remorse set in, but he soon dispelled that thought. Howard in no way wanted to sadden this happy reunion with his family. Christmas Day proved to be a very happy day, each one talking so loud and fast with the excitement of them being together again.

Elsie was a kind, loving girl and put others' happiness before her own. She and Joe had been seeing each other for sometime. Not expecting a proposal, she was happy, but surprised, when Joe slipped a ring on her finger and asked her to marry him. Her answer was "Yes, I will marry you.

"But, Joe, I will have to help Daddy with bills for awhile. With my new job, it will be easier. I can ride to work with your brother, since he goes there also. Daddy is better, but so many bills accumulated with him being sick for so long."

"Fine, Elsie, I can wait. I want you to be happy," Joe told her.

"The kids need guidance, and Daddy needs help to get him back on his feet," Elsie told Joe.

"I understand. Don't you know this is what I love about you? You are so much like your mother; she puts everyone before herself also."

As time passed, Elsie cried and sobbed in the night, and it woke the children. The children were too young to know what a hard decision she had to make. They ran to her room quickly. "Are you sick? Why are you crying? What is wrong, Elsie?"

"Nothing, nothing. There is nothing wrong with me. I have things to settle. It's a hard thing for me to do, but I will be OK. Now go back to bed."

"But we can't sleep when you cry. We want to cry, too, when we see you cry," they whimpered.

"I'm OK. Now go to bed, or you will be too tired to get up for school tomorrow. I'm fine. I am fine. I won't cry any more."

Elsie would do anything to ease the pain of her sisters and brothers. The family was so closely bound to each other that none wanted their sisters or brothers to suffer. She knew a decision had to be made. She couldn't hold off forever. She loved Joe so much, but she worried about her family.

The pressure of such a decision was devastating. Give up marrying Joe and help her daddy raise the kids. She again began to cry. This time it was a loud, uncontrollable cry.

The youngsters came running. "Do you miss Mama too, Elsie? Do you miss our mama? Is that why you are crying?"

"Yes, yes, I miss Mama an awful lot, but there are things I must think about. You don't understand, but someday you will."

After crying night after night, she made her decision. She took her ring off her finger, handed it to Joe, got out of the car, and ran into the house with out an explanation. She was too sad to stay any longer. Elsie had made her decision to help her daddy raise the family and was willing to sacrifice her own happiness and her own life for her sisters and brothers.

Joe tried over and over again to see if Elsie would change her mind. He loved her so much.

"Elsie, we can raise the three younger kids, and we will do it together. I will help you. Please marry me, Elsie."

"I can't, Oh Joe, I can't. I . . . I just can't go through with it," Elsie said, as she wiped away the tears. It was so tempting, but she knew the others would have no one to take care of them. She could not bring herself to marry Joe, since the others needed guidance and help also.

She felt this was too much to expect of a young man, to start out with four extras to feed, times being so hard, and the Great Depression still making its mark on the country would be an awful burden on him. As much as Elsie loved Joe, she felt she could not burden him with her problems. Anyway, what would happen to her other sisters and brother who had no one to care for them? Though tears were often close to the surface, she never turned away from her decision. After giving her ring back and running into the house crying, Elsie never looked back. She was afraid she might change her mind, and this she did not want to do because she knew her daddy needed help financially, as well as support in raising the younger ones.

When Elsie moved closer to her job, the younger brothers and sisters stood outside waving goodbye and crying until she was out of sight. They again felt the instability of losing someone they loved. Of course, Elsie cried also having to leave them.

The girls never had to be told to take their turn managing the household. As each left home to find work, the next in line took over the workload.

They never minded cleaning the house and caring for the others. All they wanted to do was to get the work done, so that when evening came, they would be ready for their friends to show up. Alice Grimes, Betty Anthony, Martha

Telfer, Audrey Morris, her sister, Iona, Hallie Kibble, and Betty Morris were usually the first ones to come. The family was never short of good friends.

It was no surprise to anyone that Gladys hated to cook, and she always wanted to get done in a hurry. On this particular day, she said, "I will make pancakes for your breakfast, Daddy."

"All right, but don't press down on those pancakes this time. It makes them tough."

"But, Daddy," she answered, "they will never get done, if you don't mash them down in the middle."

"They will get done, if you just give them time," Howard told her.

"OK. I'll try not to mash them in."

As she was making the pancakes, she made up a poem. She started saying her thoughts aloud. "Rosalee was a little girl, her hair was straight, without a curl. Her shoes were worn, her dress was torn. But she did not feel bad, because she was loved by Dad." Howard broke down and cried. Not wanting to be seen, he left the table and went outside until he could regain his composure.

When he came back, Gladys said, "OK, Daddy. I know I can't make good pancakes, but Alice likes our 'DeVault's hash.'"

"'DeVault's hash'? Where in the world did you come up with that name?"

"Alice calls our soup DeVault's hash. I make it kind of thick I guess. She told me she asked her mother to make some for her."

"Well," Howard said, "you must be doing a good job. We are not losing any weight. I'm kidding you. I'm glad we have this much to eat. Just a short time ago, we didn't have

~≈ The Love of Annie

food to carry in our bucket." His thoughts went back to the day he overheard a conversation between two girls discussing the day's events.

"Did you bring your lunch today?" a friend asked. "Aren't you going to eat your lunch today?"

"No, I forgot to bring my lunch," was her reply.

"I have a little more than I want, so here, you eat half of my sandwich," her friend said.

"I'm not hungry. Really, I am not hungry," the other one answered.

"I know," her friend replied, "just like I wasn't hungry that day when you shared your lunch with me." As the two friends ate their sandwich, they began to laugh. Neither had to say more. They both knew there was no lunch to forget. This conversation made Howard feel sad when he overheard the girls talking that day.

This family was so poor, but that never seemed to mar the good times they could have. One or the other found something to do to keep things in a light mood.

Anna Lee and Dixie decided they would get a bunch together and see what they could get into on Halloween night. Needless to say, they very quickly made up their minds. Anna Lee said, "Dixie, we will just throw some corn and soap a few windows; anything to jack up our time a little."

"OK," Dixie answered. "Where do we start?"

"I found some corn. Let's go!" As they were busy soaping some windows and throwing corn at a house, they heard a noise from above them.

One man decided he didn't like what these kids were doing, so he opened an upstairs window and quickly dumped the contents from his pot out of the window. The contents splattered all around, hitting them both. Of course,

Dixie was in the wrong place, so she got the biggest share of the contents on her head. They hurried home and quietly tried to wash up. Howard greeted them, trying hard not to laugh at the sight of the two girls. "My, what kind of perfume do you have on? I have smelled that somewhere before. It is such a familiar smell."

"Ah, Daddy, you know what it is. Do you know what happened?"

"Well, yes, I think I know by the way you smell."

"Daddy, he dumped the whole pot of stuff out of the upstairs window and all of it went on us."

"Well, I guess you are still lucky. He could have dropped the pot, too, you know." Each had to bathe three times to feel clean again. They thought they could still smell the contents of that pot. Often Dixie would ask, "Anna Lee, can you still smell me? I feel that I still stink."

Anna Lee said, "You smell just like you use to, and that ain't good."

"Oh, Anna Lee, tell me the truth. Do I still stink?" Dixie asked.

"Yes, but I'm used to it," Anna Lee said, with her usual good-natured humor.

"I know I don't smell any more," Dixie said as she went off to bed.

"No, Dixie, you don't smell anymore. But you don't smell any less either," Anna Lee yelled as Dixie disappeared into her room.

Chapter 25

Time after time when Howard and the children drove to the hospital to see Annie, she was glad the children came, but her twisted, sick mind kept her from being nice to Howard. She would have nothing to do with him. How he had hoped she would change her mind. Yet each time he visited Annie, she would become more upset.

When Howard tried to talk with her, she became very angry. "I told you we are through. Get out! Get out of here, and don't ever come to see me again! Do you understand? I never want to see you again," Annie said very quickly.

Feeling helpless, Howard sat with tears welling up inside of him. How he hoped his Annie would change and at least talk with him.

When the time came they had to leave, Howard waited silently, hoping she would say something . . . anything. But Annie would not look at him. He felt so sad; it literally broke his heart. He wanted so badly to hear a kind word or at least for her to tell him goodbye. Howard went home feeling more depressed; his hopes again shattered. But Annie loved to see her oldest son Johnny when he came to visit her, though he didn't go very often. As the years went by, he would go to see her less and less.

By now Johnny suffered from a disease in his lungs, and his health was failing. He had black lung disease from breathing too much black dust in the coal mines. His lungs were so full of black dust, he could barely get enough air to keep going. He'd cough so long with out being able to breathe, anyone who stood within earshot wanted to breathe for him himself. Anything to get air into his lungs. "Johnny, how I wish I could help you," they would say.

As Johnny gasped for air, he'd make a gesture with his hand as if to say, "No one can do anything to help me. I have to face this by myself."

No one told Annie her oldest son was slowly dying. They wanted to protect her from the awful pain she would feel if she knew her beloved son would also die from working in the coal mines. The mines had taken the lives of her husband Carper, her brother Guy, and her precious Howard had broken his back in the mines.

The family feared all the old memories and hurt might come to the surface again if they told her Johnny, too, was dying. They didn't want to bring her more pain or sorrow. So Johnny chose to stay away to protect his mama from seeing him fighting for air.

Annie thought her son was so busy trying to support his wife and family that she accepted the fact he didn't come to see her as often. But she missed him, and Johnny felt just as sad at not seeing her.

One afternoon Howard again went to the hospital to see his Annie. While waiting for her to be brought to the visiting area, he heard someone call his name, "Mr. DeVault, I'm Doctor Brown. I feel I must talk to you."

"Yes, Doctor, what is it?"

"I must talk to you about your wife."

"Is there any change in my wife? Is she any better?"

"No, Mr. DeVault, I'm afraid not. She gets so agitated when you come to visit her that I suggest you don't come anymore for awhile. I know this hurts, but I must be honest with you. If she changes her mind and asks for you, I will let you know immediately. But for the time being, it would be best if you didn't come to see her for sometime."

Howard's head dropped. Annie had been away so long. He hoped it would help her to know how much he still loved her, and in turn she would at least talk with him.

"Mr. DeVault, this happens all the time. When someone has a mental breakdown, or what we refer to as a nervous breakdown, they turn against the one they love the most. It's hard to understand this type of behavior, but that's the way it is. I'm terribly sorry to have to tell you this. As sad as it may seem, it is true. I'm sorry. Her chances of getting better are much better if she doesn't get overly agitated."

"Well, Doctor, I'm sure you know what is best for her. I'll not come for awhile. Maybe this will help her. How I hope so. She is my whole life. I will do anything to make her better."

"Yes, I can see you care for her very deeply. Just remember, Howard, when she gets better things will change."

"Thank you," Howard said as he turned and walked to the car.

After several months had passed and Howard was still not allowed to see Annie, he decided to write her a note. The children made a picnic dinner to take to their mama.

The Love of Annie

As they were getting into the car Howard slipped a folded note into one of their hands, hoping Annie would read it.

"Please give this note to Mom for me, will you?"

"Yes, Daddy, we will see that Mama gets it."

"Thank you, but please be sure to see that she gets it, will you?"

"Yes, Daddy, we will give it to her. We promise we will give it to Mama."

There were very few words on the note. It read: "Mom, I miss you. If I can come to see you, please let one of the children know. I love you and I want to see you. Please let me know if you want to see me. Love, Howard."

Howard had made several more attempts to see his Annie, but nothing seemed to work. She was oblivious to what was going on around her, especially where Howard was concerned.

After Annie had been hospitalized for several years, the children wanted her to come home again. Because she had suffered so much poverty and hurt from the death and injury of her loved ones in the coal mines, they felt strongly that coming back to a nicer home, a better environment, and a loving family, would be beneficial to her mental health. Years in the hospital had not helped her much. Perhaps the answer was to be with her beloved family again, back with her children who wanted her home so badly. Annie's doctor agreed it was worth a try, since the children wanted to give her all they could.

Elsie thought she should go back home to be with Mama, and so she could help the family again. She quit her job to be there when Annie came from the hospital, and she began work at a local grocery store.

The Love of Annie

After the papers were filled out, Annie came home, and Howard was truly elated to see her. But Annie did not pay any attention to him. She was no better, and the new home and surroundings didn't seem to help at all. The older children were gone; only the four younger ones were home yet.

Although the love the children had for Annie was deep, in a few months it was obvious they had let their love and emotions be their guide, rather than common sense. Annie could not bring herself to be interested in things around her. She sat alone the biggest part of the day. Eventually, she began to walk to the post office and grocery store much too often. She would stop along the way, say a few words to someone, and hurry back home. Shortly afterward, she would go back. She seemed to be looking for something special at the post office—some piece of mail, package, a check, or something. Whatever it was, no one knew. When it became obvious that Annie had not improved, everyone suffered heartbreak again, knowing they would have to take their precious mama back to the hospital and away from her family.

On the day Annie was to go back to the institution, Howard called the youngest children together and said, "Anna Lee, I want to tell you and Dixie something. Mom is not any better, so we have to get more help for her. They will be coming today to take her back to the hospital. We all love her so much, but she still needs help. We have to give Mama a chance now, don't we?"

"Yes, Daddy, we understand. We have to try to get Mama all better. We do have to give her a chance. But it hurts, Daddy, it hurts so bad. How I wish we could keep Mama home. It doesn't seem fair for her to have to live somewhere else, Daddy."

"No, honey, it isn't fair, but we can't do anything about it. Try to understand that we are doing it to get more help for her, so that she can live a decent life like other people do."

"We will, Daddy."

When Anna Lee left for school that day, her mind was working overtime, and her heart was breaking. She mounted the school bus without speaking to anyone. Her thoughts were all of her mama. She went to her classes in a daze. Finally, in the third-period history class, she completely lost control of her emotions and began crying uncontrollably.

"What is wrong, Anna Lee?" the teacher asked. "Tell me, why are you so upset? Anna Lee! Anna Lee! Listen to me. We want to help you."

Anna Lee couldn't get her emotions under control. She was a young teenager, and the pain was too much for her. Her memory went back to when she was six years old and two policemen took her mama away. Now Mama's leaving broke her heart all over again. She couldn't accept it. Finally, Anna Lee was so distraught, she had to be taken out of the classroom and given a sedative. It was a couple days before she could return to school. Howard tried with all the love he had to explain to her what had happened. But her love for Annie never lessened; it seemed to grow stronger as the months passed.

Each of her children felt the pain of losing their mama all over again when she was taken from them. It again broke their hearts.

Taking Mama back to the hospital was extremely hard on the children, each was a little older now and each had a little more understanding.

By now her children knew and understood their mama's life was a sad one. Her life could not be happy. And each of them knew she would rather be at home, rather than going back to the hospital. The pain of losing her again was devastating to this loving family.

Gladys realized her mama was in a psychopathic ward in a mental hospital. It bothered her terribly. The pain was so bad she could not begin to accept it either. She had the lead part in the senior class play and wanted so badly to do well. One of her lines was: "If this keeps up, I will end up in some psychopathic ward." Those words were too much for her to even think about, much less to say aloud. She felt so hurt that her mama had to live like this. Without even realizing what she had done, she made up her own words. Luckily, Bill Campbell picked up his cue and went on without a moment of hesitation. No one knew the difference except those two and the play director. Gladys was so relieved that she got through those two lines that she readily apologized for her mistake. She had memorized the entire play, but the hurt of her mama being in a psychopathic ward was so devastating that she could not remember those few words. She had completely blocked them from her mind.

After Annie went back to the institution, Howard told the children, "I know this is so sad for you all. I'm hurting too, but Mom would feel worse, if she knew her illness has caused us so much pain. Now I want you to go on living your life to the fullest. You will still have a lot of pain and hurting, but you are too young to carry such a load. I think you should have as much fun as you can while we are all still close to each other. Soon enough you may be scattered in different directions."

The Love of Annie

When the children took a box of candy to Annie, Howard wrote another note and sneaked it into the candy, thinking she would be sure to find it. But someone ate all of the candy, except a couple of pieces, so Annie never found his note. It had read: "Mom, if you would like for me to come out to see you, tell Elsie, so she can let me know." Feeling so hopeless, his last note was just these few simple words and was signed, "I love you, Howard."

It wouldn't have made any difference if Annie had found his note or not, she was very ill and did not want to see or hear from Howard. Yet he continued to hope she would love him again sometime in the future. Each time someone was making the trip to the hospital to see her, Howard, with tears in his eyes and his voice wavering, would say, "Tell Mom I miss her, and wish I could be there." But there was never a response from his Annie.

As each of the children married and had their own homes, Howard became even more lonely and desolate. When the last child married, his loneliness was unbearable. Twenty-five long years he had waited and waited and prayed for his Annie to get well and to love him again. But there was never any change. If anything, Annie became even more bitter. His notes always went unnoticed and unanswered. His very last note was only, "I loved you so much, Mom, and I will always long to see you. Love, Howard."

To overcome his loneliness, Howard tried to keep busy, but it wasn't enough. He worked hard and tried to pay all the bills he had owed for so many years. He owed money to a dentist for so long, and Howard was determined to be honest in any dealings he had made. When he went to pay his bill, the dentist said, "Howard, you don't owe me any money. I don't have a record of it." Howard answered, "No, I'm sure you don't have a record of my bill, but I do." He paid his bill, thanked the dentist, then left.

Howard was so lonely. After a few months had passed, he met a lady who was as lonely as he was. They talked whenever they could. It eased some of their loneliness.

His two older children encouraged their daddy to try to find a little life of his own. It was a fact that after all these years, Annie could not get well enough to be with Howard or to even talk with him. The children hoped their daddy could find a wee bit of contentment in his life and curtail a little of the loneliness he experienced. They felt that if he had found someone who was compatible, he deserved to have some one to at least talk to. The relationship was not for love; it was only to curtail a little of his loneliness. Howard needed someone to make his long nights go a little faster and fill in the empty feeling he had suffered for so long.

Johnny and Ruthie talked with their minister. They wanted to handle this delicate situation in a Christian way. The minister said some would pronounce this situation as an absolution. And because Annie had never recovered, and her illness changed her love to such a profound hate toward Howard, he gave Howard his blessings. Only God knows and understands this particular illness.

After seeing each other for some time, Howard and Mary decided they should get married. *At least we will have each other to go places with and some one to fill in the long evenings and nights,* they thought. Within a few weeks, they settled down in their own home. Neither found true love or happiness in this union, but each made the best of the situation.

Annie forever hovered in Howard's mind. He'd remember the picnics with all of the children at the Webster schoolhouse on the Fourth of July and the big watermelon, which was kept in a huge tub of cold water until the picnic started. He also thought of their rabbit hunting escapades and the Halloween capers they pulled on the town children. Of course his favorite memories were the different antics that went on with their own children.

A few special ones would always bring a smile to his face: The time Bobby threw Gladys into the rain barrel when he got tired of watching her; when Billy cut off all of Anna Lee's hair (after that, Anna Lee picked up the nickname, "Peeled Onion," and it stayed with her until she was a young lady); when Ethel fell head first into the pig pen; and when Viola (there was always something happening with her) got into the yellow jackets' nest, or when she fell out of the swing and ending up being hospitalized for so long because her appendix had burst.

When Howard heard Betty, Martha, and Gladys laughing as they stood under the street light every night, he wondered what they could possibly find to laugh that hard about. These were always special times in Howard's life, as were the summer picnics. Howard loved every picnic they ever had. Picnics were his happiest times.

Thinking of all these things kept his Annie alive in his memory. He thought back to when their first child was born. It was still so vivid in his mind. His memories were too precious for him to erase. So often when he was alone, his thoughts wandered back to those good old days with his Annie.

Chapter 26

One March day, in 1963, Howard wrote a letter to his daughter who lived in Minnesota. It read as follows: "March 21. It's supposed to be the first day of spring, and it looks more like the first day of winter.

"I am going to tell you the truth, when an old buzzard has passed the three score and ten mark, it is time to start on the downhill side. So don't be surprised when you get the call. Right now I do not have an ache or a pain anyplace, but I will be seventy-one on my next birthday. If you can, take a vacation this summer, and come home. Will say goodbye. Love to all, Dad."

As the months went by and summer came, Howard visited every one of his children just one week before he was found, collapsed at the bottom of the stairs. He was rushed to the hospital and was found to be in a coma, either from when he fell or soon afterwards. Very quickly, the doctors asked a lot of questions as to why he was found at the bottom of the steps.

The Love of Annie

They did every thing they could to make him comfortable, even though there was not much they could do to bring him out of the coma. Howard's children stayed by his side constantly watching, praying, hoping, and waiting for his recovery. More than anything else, they wanted any sign that he would be OK, but he only seemed to get weaker.

After a couple of weeks had gone by, the children were worried. Although Howard tried to hold on to his life, it was still slowly slipping away from his grasp.

More questions were asked about his fall. They asked if he had been pushed down the stairs and who was in the home at the time of the accident. There was no decision as to what had caused him to fall and land at the bottom of the steps. The doctors said he had a cerebral hemorrhage, but whether this caused the fall or not, remained to be seen. He had never caused trouble for anyone in his life when he was well. Now that he was sick, he surely would not want any trouble for anyone. Howard was a peace-loving person. His children left well enough alone and did not check it any further. Although he was so ill, the love for his family still showed in his eyes. All his suffering could not block out the deep love he felt for his loved ones.

All the children lived close by except Gladys. "I think he wants to see her," they commented. *Or maybe Mama too,* they thought. *It seems he is trying so hard to hold on to his life.* Each child took a turn being with their daddy as much as possible during his last days. They felt strongly that he was hoping to see his beloved Annie once more—just once more before he died.

Gladys flew home to be with her daddy. He roused from the coma he was in when she leaned over his bed. He lifted his head from the pillow to kiss his loving daughter seven times. She was so happy that he knew her and knew that she had come home to be with him. She spent as much time with him as possible.

Now that she was home, the children knew Howard had seen everyone that he wanted to see. Yes, every one—everyone, except his beloved Annie.

One day, while Gladys was sitting quietly in a chair at the foot of his bed, a very small lady came in. She was about the size of his Annie before she became ill and had to go away. This lady looked straight ahead and walked toward Howard. She stood very still for a moment, then leaned over very closely to his face, as though she were going to whisper something to him or kiss him. She looked down into his pale face and gently rubbed his forehead. She cupped both of her hands on his face, oh, so tenderly, just as Annie had done with Howard many years before. She turned and walked out of the hospital room without a single word. She looked straight ahead and did not even glance toward Gladys as she left. Gladys wondered why this beautiful, kind lady did not speak to her, at least smile at her, or say something to Howard, since he was awake and had been looking up into her face.

Gladys normally would have been quick to say something to the visitor, but for some reason, the opportunity had not presented itself. The loving tenderness the lady displayed to her daddy was unbelievable. Gladys thought this beautiful lady must have been a very dear friend or a relative whom perhaps she could not remember. The loving way she had about her had been so noticeable. Gladys could not help but wonder why she hadn't looked her way as she walked away from his bed or at least cast a smile as she left. It seemed odd, since a hospital room generally promotes kindness. And not saying one word to Howard as she patted him on his face so lovingly. Displaying such devotion to him was yet more puzzling.

As Howard lay dying, barely able to mutter a word, barely able to speak at all, he asked, "Who . . . was . . . that . . . there? Mom? Was . . . that . . . Mom?"

"I didn't know her, Daddy," Gladys answered, ever so softly. "I thought she must have been a friend of yours from back here in Ohio."

Howard again asked, oh so very slowly, "Who . . . was . . . that . . . there . . . Mom? Was . . . that . . . Mom? Mom?"

Gladys knew how badly he wanted it to be his Annie, so she said, "Bob is out in the hall, Daddy." She hoped "Bob" would sound to him like "Mom"—the word he so much wanted to hear.

When he began to ask for the third time if it was Mom, his daughter quickly said, "Bob is still out in the hall, Daddy. I will step out so someone else can come in to see you. We don't want you to get overtired." Bob came in to see Howard, just as he slipped back into a coma.

When Bob came out of the room later, Gladys asked him who the lady was who came to see Daddy. "Daddy thought it was Mama," she said.

"Gladys," Bob said, "there was no woman here. There wasn't anyone in the hall. Nobody has been here since you went in to see Daddy. Gert and I were standing square in front of the door, so no woman could come down the hall without one of us seeing her. And she sure couldn't have gone through the door without us noticing her, because we'd have had to move out of her way. Believe me, there was no one but us here since you went into Daddy's room."

The Love of Annie

The children who were present at that time tried to find an explanation concerning this lady. Again, Gladys told them how lovingly she had treated Daddy.

"I knew that Daddy thought it was Mama," Gladys said. "She was such a loving lady, and she seemed to care so much for him. She kept touching him and patting him on his forehead."

"Well, there in fact was no one but ourselves in the hall since you went in," they said.

Because the end of the hall had no doors except the one to Howard's room, they couldn't explain how this lady had gotten there. Each claimed that absolutely no one came past them. Yet two people saw this lady. Two people saw this strange phenomenon, both Gladys and Howard himself, who had asked two times, "Who was that?" He was about to ask again the third time, but, Gladys, noticing her daddy was having such a hard time getting the words out because of his weakness and frail breathing, said, "Bob is just by the door in the hall, Daddy." She hoped he'd take *Bob* for *Mom*.

It seemed really strange that two people saw this phenomenon, yet those by the door waiting for their turn to be with Howard, did not see anyone. We can only hope that through God's tender loving mercy, he sent an angel in Annie's stead, so that Howard could feel her presence once more. . . . just once more before he died.

Chapter 27

Annie did recover from her mental illness, but it was too late—too late to tell Howard that she still loved him. It was too late for Howard to know she did recover from the devastating illness. And it was too late for him to touch her and hold her in his arms one more time, as he had longed to do for so many years. It was also too late for Annie to let him know that she still loved the ring that he had given her so long ago.

One day Annie asked, "Do you know where my wedding ring is, Elsie?"

"Yes, Mama, I have kept it for you all of these years. It is at our house. When you want it, I will bring it to you."

"Could I please have my wedding band now if you have time, Elsie? I would love to have my ring, if I could."

"Of course, Mama. I will bring it to you right away."

"Thank you, Elsie. I always loved my ring. I was sick—very sick—wasn't I?"

The Love of Annie

"Yes, Mama, you were sick. We loved you so much all that time. I think we loved you all the more, Mama, because of the tornado and the terrible Depression, and what it did to our family. It is so good to have you well again," Elsie told her Mama as she stood with her arms around her shoulder.

"It is so nice to be able to talk with you and to hug you, Mama. We are happy to have you home with us now."

Annie reached for Elsie's hand and smiled sweetly, knowing that she was still very much needed to fulfill the lives of her children.

Realizing that so many years had passed, Annie asked about Howard and about his death. By the smile on her face, and the fact that she wanted her ring back, the kids all knew she still loved her Howard.

"You said I was ill for some time. How long was I sick, Elsie?"

"Mama, you have been fighting this for many years. It wasn't fair, Mama, but when you first became ill, the medicine they had was not very good. The doctors did all they could for you. Today the medicine is so much better than it was back when you first had this problem. You see, Mama, now you are better, and you can be home with us. That's all that matters now. You are better."

"Yes, honey. I feel alive again now."

Annie was only out of the state hospital a short time before she became very ill. She had an examination, and when it was finished, the report was bad, very bad. The doctor said she had cancer, and it had spread very quickly through her body—so fast, in fact, they did not know where it had started.

When the doctor told Elsie and Gert, their brother's wife, the news that their mama was so sick, the thought of it

The Love of Annie

broke Elsie's heart. Just when they had their mama home with them, too quickly Elsie felt the hurt of having to give her up once more. It was hard for Elsie to hold back her tears in front of the doctor, though she tried. How it hurt the rest of the children when they were told about their mama being so ill.

Annie was still the same beautiful Annie she'd been long ago. She never complained or felt sorry for herself. No one ever knew when Annie was not feeling good, because her concern was for others so much of the time.

Once more, Annie asked the children about Howard. It seemed she had to know all she could, as if she realized how much grief her illness had been to so many of those she loved.

Shortly after this, the doctor called the children to her bedside. As they hurried to her room one of the sisters noticed her brother Johnny was far behind. She ran back to find him gasping for air. He had tried to keep up the fast pace of the others to get to his Mama's bedside, but couldn't because of his lung disease. She took his hand, and they walked slowly to where Mama lay dying.

Annie was alert and knew all of her children were with her. A blood clot was headed to her heart, and there was no way the doctors could stop it. She was too sick herself to notice that Johnny was also very ill, and he, too, would be dying before very long.

Annie slowly lifted her hand to touch each of her children for the last time as they stood beside her. Once more, with her still sweet loving smile, the smile that no one could ever forget, she looked lovingly at each of them. The children tried to hold back their tears, so Mama would not see the pain they felt at losing her once more. *Mama's suffering*

~~ The Love of Annie

will soon be all over, they thought as they waited by her bedside. This gave each of them a little comfort, but their love for their mama was so deep within each of them, they still hated to see her go.

The nurse came in and told them she had to change something, to make Annie rest a little better, so they left her room for a short time. Some of the family had to go home to check on other members of their family. They hoped they could be back in time to see her again, but all too soon, her breathing became very slow. The blood clot had traveled very fast to her heart. The doctor announced once more, it was only a matter of time she would be with them. The children, with a prayer on their lips and a hurt in their hearts, stood waiting and watching. They knew Mama was soon going away once more, at long last, to have peace . . . a peace she had never known before.

Within a few hours, Annie died, and she took her wedding band with her to the grave . . . along with her never-ending love for her Howard.

Annie died on June 20, 1975 at the age of 85.
Howard passed away on August 1, 1963 at the age of 71.
Johnny died on October 7, 1983.

Our Last Letter

As we are writing this last letter, it's the merry month of June.
The birds are sweetly singing, all nature seems in tune.
Mama, how you would love it, if you were here today.
You could walk the hills and valleys, and pick flowers on the way.

The grass along the river banks is such a vivid green.
We know you would love it; it's the prettiest we have seen.
Mama, the woods are gorgeous, fallen trees are very few.
It almost takes your breath away, as the woods come into view.

One more thing we'll tell you, it is something we must say.
We loved you so much Mama, because you taught us how to pray.
When He wanted one in heaven, it was you who Jesus chose.
He knew He picked an angel, or at least a lovely rose.

Well, Mama, we just wanted to be close to you once more.
The hills, the woods and valleys are what you loved before.
Now this is our last letter, as your soul flits through the sky.
We love you still, and always will, now we must say good-bye.

In Memory of Our Mother, Annie,
From Her Children

To order additional copies of

THE LOVE OF ANNIE

send $12.95 plus shipping and handling to

**Books Etc.
PO Box 4888
Seattle, WA 98104**

or have your credit card ready and call

(800) 917-BOOK